The Secrets Necklace

The Secrets Necklace

Jessie Paddock

Scholastic Inc.

Copyright © 2019 by Jessie Paddock

All rights reserved. Published by Scholastic Inc., *Publishers since 1920*. SCHOLASTIC and associated logos are trademarks and/or registered trademarks of Scholastic Inc.

The publisher does not have any control over and does not assume any responsibility for author or third-party websites or their content.

This book is a work of fiction. Names, characters, places, and incidents are either the product of the author's imagination or are used fictitiously, and any resemblance to actual persons, living or dead, business establishments, events, or locales is entirely coincidental.

ISBN 978-1-338-57104-2

10 9 8 7 6 5 4 3 2 1   19 20 21 22 23

Printed in the U.S.A.   40

First printing 2019

Book design by Yaffa Jaskoll

For Dan Carlisle Jr.

Chapter One

Three things happened to Penny Hoppe on August 30. Well, not just three things. Plenty of other things, too. Regular stuff like brushing her teeth, frantically trying to tame her unruly bangs, slowly scrambling eggs for breakfast, and waving goodbye to her pet lizards. All normal, average occurrences proceeded without interruption. But there were three things that morning that proved especially significant. Life changingly significant, in fact.

First, her older brother, Otis, moved two hours away to Atlanta to take a job cooking at a fancy-shmancy, don't-eat-with-your-hands kind of restaurant.

Second, it was the first day of seventh grade—a grade Penny hadn't been particularly looking forward to but, up until her alarm clock went off, hadn't been dreading, either.

Third, Penny started sneezing.

Correction: Penny started sneezing when she was nervous. It was an odd and inconvenient symptom. The trait did not run in the family; it was a quality entirely Penny's own.

Penny had a sneaking suspicion all three of the major things that happened that day were related, but she didn't quite know how to put them together yet. They were all quite perplexing in their own ways. But that didn't matter. Understanding the three major things wouldn't change anything. Otis was gone, school was in session, and Penny couldn't stop sneezing her butt off.

As the first two weeks of school went by, Penny found herself wishing for an instruction manual that laid out the steps to surviving middle school—a recipe she could follow, like the ones she used to make chocolate chip cookies, chicken pot pie, or pancakes. A How to Survive Seventh Grade Without Your BFF/Older Brother recipe. If only seventh grade were more like cooking, she'd be in great shape because, just like her older brother, Penny could cook. Correction: Penny could follow a recipe, and as far as Penny knew, cooking and recipe-following were basically the same thing.

So when Penny's nose started to tingle at 9:04 a.m., at the end of her poetry class, she knew what to expect. Sort of.

Penny's desk was in the second row all the way to the right. Penny was short for her age, possibly the shortest seventh grader at Lullwater Middle School, and her shoes barely touched the floor. She tapped the toes of her sneakers against the ground, *pit-pat*, *pit-pat*.

"We have time for one more reader," Ms. Samich announced.

Penny felt a tingle in the very tip of her nose, like a distant star coming to life, a stray spark from a bonfire, or the first freckle of summer. Then another, and then another. Tingle, spark, spark, tingle, spark.

"Don't all volunteer at once, now," Ms. Samich added, chuckling at her own joke. The class was silent.

Ms. Samich came to Mr. Turney's English class once a week to teach poetry. She was a flustered lady; there was more hair out of her bun than in it, she had a habit of saying things that *almost* made sense, and she carried with her a massive bag that seemed to contain everything from colored pencils to water bottles to folders and folders of general documents. But despite her ridiculous name and her overwhelmed appearance, Penny liked Ms. Samich.

See, Ms. Samich had introduced Penny to poetry, and to Penny Hoppe, writing poetry felt like spilling a too-long-kept secret. In other words, poetry was a relief. Penny found she could write things on the page that she'd never consider admitting out loud. Ms. Samich's visits were the best part of seventh grade so far. Excluding the five minutes at the end of class when Ms. Samich asked for volunteers to share their writing aloud. Penny felt like that was a positively unnecessary part of the whole writing-beautiful-poems thing. Poetry was supposed to be private—something to be sealed in a box, meant for the creator's enjoyment alone.

Penny did not sneeze when writing poetry. However, the mere thought of reading her poem aloud sent a geyser of sparks and tingles from the tip of her nose into her sinuses.

Ms. Samich paced in front of the class patiently. Despite her frazzled demeanor, her movement was almost menacing. "Any brave volunteers?"

Silence.

"Going once . . ."

Without moving her head a millimeter, Penny darted her eyes around the classroom. She didn't want to draw any unnecessary attention to herself, but the sparks and tingles building in her nose threatened to blow her cover. Couldn't someone else just suck it up and raise their hand so this horrible waiting game would be over with and they could all just go about their days? The absolute last thing on earth Penny Hoppe wanted to do was volunteer to read her poem.

"Going twice . . ."

"I can read my other piece," Mateo announced from the seat directly in front of Penny. Mateo always volunteered. It didn't matter what class. He'd been volunteering nonstop since third grade. The poem he'd read to the class just a few minutes earlier described an anticlimactic part of his favorite video game in very generic detail. Snoozefest.

"I'd like to give someone who we haven't heard from yet a chance," Ms. Samich answered. Ms. Samich, along with basically every other teacher who ever lived, had that very sneaky teacherlike habit of calling on the one unlucky kid who did not want to be seen. Penny sank a little lower in her chair. Only the top half of her eyeballs and her bangs remained above the horizon of her desk.

Spark, tingle, spark, tingle.

Not breathing was one of the more scientifically proven ways to squelch an oncoming sneeze of epic proportions. Which was exactly what was building in Penny's nose: a tropical storm of a sneeze. And if the storm made landfall, Ms. Samich would without a doubt notice her.

"Remember, y'all: Our final presentation is fast approaching. Which I'm delighted to say, for those of you who don't remember, will be a poetry reading!" A lot of strange things delighted Ms. Samich. "A big part of writing, and art-making in general, is sharing your work—and yourself—with the world. Right now is a fabulous time to practice before you get onstage."

She continued to pace around the room and the class continued to ignore her plea for volunteers. Ms. Samich just would not give up.

"And remember, all of your work is still in progress. It's okay if it doesn't feel perfect or final yet."

Tingle, tingle, spark, tingle.

Penny looked down at her poem again. On her

first day, Ms. Samich gave every student what she called a poetry journal—a special notebook just for her class. Clearly homemade with pieces of copy paper folded and stapled, Penny loved hers all the same. Ms. Samich instructed everyone to write their names clearly on the front, but Penny couldn't help but write *Chef* on the cover in bright purple marker. *Why not?* she'd thought.

They'd been composing drafts of "Where I'm From" poems for the last two classes. Her precise handwriting spelled out twelve lines and three stanzas so far. Even her title was evocative, simultaneously mysterious and enticing. But after Mateo's video game poem, and Cole's pathetic attempt at rhyming before that, Penny considered the possibility that she'd misunderstood the assignment. According to Ms. Samich, poetry was all about writing what your heart feels (another instruction that *almost* made sense). Had Penny completely misread her own heart?

Spark, spark.

"Last chance, young artists . . ."

Penny's eyes watered and she felt her breath catch in the back of her throat. She had the distinct sensation that she'd swallowed a small balloon. Tropical storm officially upgraded to hurricane status. Spark. Spark. Spark. Category-two hurricane in full effect.

"Speak now or forever hold your peace—and by forever I mean until next class, when we indulge this whole charade again." Ms. Samich took a step in Penny's direction.

Did Penny have a bull's-eye on her forehead or something?

Spark, spark.

Penny managed to shrink a little lower in her seat. The bone at the base of her neck bore into the back of her plastic chair. Her poor nose fizzed and tingled. Her eyes watered and her vision blurred. There was nothing she could do to stop it now. Penny rushed her hands to her face to stifle the explosion.

"Ahhh-*choo!*"

Penny's sneeze rumbled and shook her whole body, generating extreme power. Her chest jerked downward, thrusting her desk forward, knocking into the back of Mateo's chair.

"What the—" Mateo said.

At least momentarily, Penny felt better. No more tingles, no more sparks. No boogers had been harmed or released in the making of the sneeze. She blinked and slightly shook her head to reorient herself as she sat back up.

Only then did she notice her missing poetry journal.

Frantically, she scanned her surroundings. Had she sneezed every page into dust?

No, not dust. Her poetry journal sat smack in the middle of the aisle, two desk lengths in front of her, page open, all twelve lines and three stanzas faceup and available for the entire world to see. It rested on the ground right beside Gianna King's perfectly double-knotted sneaker.

"Man down!" Penny screamed as she leaped forward to interrupt. After many years of playing pool basketball with Otis, Penny knew how to dive for an object that seemed nearly out of reach. Screaming nonsense while you did it only made it more fun.

Penny crashed to the ground, poetry journal safely in her outstretched hands, before anybody had a chance to see any of the precious twelve lines, three stanzas. The skin on her elbows burned as they squeaked against the floor, but Penny didn't care. Her words, her poem, and her heart were safe.

"Crisis averted," she whispered.

Penny heard Ms. Samich's voice from behind. "Quite the dramatic entrance, Penny H."

"That's me," Penny admitted as she scrambled to her feet. She didn't realize Ms. Samich knew her name. Her first name *and* her last initial. Had her rugby-style nosedive been a bit dramatic? She glanced at her classmates. Some stifled laughs. Some did not stifle their laughs. Janiyah and Jane, the identical twins in the front row, looked identically frightened.

"Ooh, that's gonna leave a mark!" Cole shouted from the back row. Ugh. Cole's jokes were so elementary school.

Penny darted her eyes back to Gianna to catch her reaction. She sat perfectly composed at her desk, not a hair in her two French braids out of place, hands in lap, as if completely immune to the fact that a crazed girl had just launched herself across the room screaming in order to retrieve a notebook.

It did not make Penny feel good to be ignored by Gianna King.

"The stage is yours, Penny H." Ms. Samich now stood at the back of the room leaning against that dumb poster that said KEEP CALM AND LOVE 7TH GRADE LANGUAGE ARTS. "We're excited to hear your work."

Ms. Samich always called writing *work*. Even if it was a free write, even if it was a sentence that made no sense, even if it was just a doodle. Penny kind of liked that. It made her feel professional. And on this disastrously sneezy day, it gave Penny just the boost of confidence she needed to remain at the front of class. Though for a moment she considered alley-ooping her way right out the door.

"Okay," Penny said. Squeaked, rather. Ms. Samich nodded and Penny scurried her eyes to the ground. Reality set in. Penny Lorraine Hoppe, all four foot, eight inches of her, stood in front of her class clutching a homemade poetry journal that contained the most true and the most private combination of letters and words. Penny blinked. Then blinked again. Her eyes remained laser focused on the ground. She raised her journal. Then a little higher. And a little higher. And just a few inches higher and . . . perfect! Her view of her classmates was entirely blocked!

"Your poetry journal isn't a mask, my dear. Lower it, please, so we can see your face," Penny heard Ms. Samich call.

"And hear you," Mateo added. Yes, Mateo volunteered public speaking tips, too. So bossy.

Penny slowly peeked over the top edge of the page. Ms. Samich grinned back. Along with the faces of twenty-five of her classmates. Like a scary movie she couldn't tear her eyes away from, Penny couldn't stop herself from peering around the room once again. That was a mistake. A big, big mistake.

The boys toward the back got her attention first. T.C. had his fingers lodged deep in the mess of his very curly and very poufy hair, as if digging for treasure. Max appeared as if he were mouthing the words to a song. His eyes were glazed over but not closed. Theo sat behind them, staring straight at Penny with what surely had to be a devilish look in his eye. Cole flicked the eraser side of a pencil inside his cheek. His braces glimmered in the harsh overhead light. *Unsanitary*, Penny thought. The girl who always had gigantic lime green headphones around her neck doodled in her notebook, absorbed in another world entirely, it seemed. Gianna gently coughed, of course making sure to cover her mouth with her hand.

"Treat this as a rehearsal. Remember to introduce yourself and say the title of your work before you start."

Penny took a deep breath. "I'm Penny Hoppe," she said. Why did her full name suddenly sound so ridiculous when said out loud? Like the name of a doll or a dolphin at the zoo. Did everybody else think her name was ridiculous? She couldn't quite tell. Based on the blank slash bored looks on her classmates' faces, there was a good possibility.

"Louder, Dimes!" Cole called from the back row. Ugh, why did he always call her that? So not inventive.

Tingle.

Laughter filtered through the class. After a few seconds, a blanket of chatter covered the room. Penny looked toward Ms. Samich, who still leaned against the back wall. Why didn't Ms. Samich say anything to hush the class? How could she let this happen?

"I'm Penny Hoppe," Penny repeated.

Spark.

"And this is called—"

Tingle. Category-four storm, gaining strength.

Penny blinked back the liquid forming in the inside corners of her eyes. Yes, she was blinking too much. She was positive. Penny thought, *Now Gianna and everyone will think I'm trying not to cry!* Penny didn't know much, but she was certain that crying in front of your class while giving an oral presentation of sorts was not considered cool.

Penny's hands trembled. The bottom of her feet felt clammy in her sneakers.

"Now or never," a voice called. Maybe Theo, maybe Max.

Penny opened her mouth to speak. She took the biggest breath she could muster, but the air came in ragged gulps, as if passing through the smallest holes on a cheese grater. She glanced at her paper just to confirm she knew the title of her poem. Of course she knew it. It was hers. There was nothing left to do but start . . .

But Penny's voice just wouldn't come out. Her nose tingled and sparked and tingled and sparked, and she stared at her classmates, frozen. Well, her body froze like unthawed ice cream. Her brain, however, felt like rapidly boiling water waiting for a handful of rigatoni to cook.

Penny was spiraling, and spiraling fast.

Then, in a tone that reminded Penny of an alligator, Mateo offered, "I'll read it for her."

Penny blushed and she jerked her poetry journal tight to her chest. Her poem was not Mateo's to read.

"Actually," Penny interjected, finally finding her voice, "I'm not. I mean I can't. Not today. No way. No thank you."

And then, maybe because her cheeks were bright red and her eyes burned, not from an oncoming sneeze, but kind of, maybe, sort of because she was about to cry and she had to conceal her face ASAP, or maybe because at the end of the day Penny was just a bit theatrical, she took a grand bow. She heard one stray clap from the back of the room.

Penny scuttled her sneezy self to her seat. Yes, an instruction manual with a recipe for surviving the most humiliating public speaking fail of all time would have been really helpful.

Once seated, Penny kept her poetry journal hugged to her body. Her toes pitty-patted the floor at the same tempo as her explosive heartbeat. Even though her feet easily reached the ground, Penny suddenly felt much shorter than four foot eight.

"Next time," Penny thought she heard Ms. Samich say, though she couldn't be sure. Penny didn't dare look up, but she felt the weight of twenty-five sets of eyes on her, judging, ridiculing, and doing all the other scary and mysterious things seventh graders tended to do.

"Okay, so as you all know, or as you all should know—I'm talking to you, T.C., Max, and Theo"—Ms. Samich had a sixth sense for those not paying attention—"our end-of-semester performance will be in the auditorium."

Spark, tingle.

Ms. Samich continued, "The entire middle school is invited. Your families are invited. Your long-lost friends and pets are invited. Everyone will have the opportunity to share one piece of work." The students started to rustle as the clock on the wall indicated class was over. Actually, class had been over for thirty seconds. An eternity in seventh-grade time. "Beautiful job today, everyone. See you next week."

Penny watched her classmates immediately start

chatting, whooping, and, in Cole's case, flexing his arm muscles. Between-period pandemonium. She sat at her desk another moment and pit-patted her feet one last time. Her nose didn't tingle, she could take a deep breath with ease, and she didn't have that feeling in her mouth like she'd swallowed a balloon. The relief only lasted a few moments.

Penny had chickened out. And, as she was starting to learn, the feeling of chickening out was maybe worse than all the tidal-wave sneezes combined. Penny stood to leave and stashed her petite poetry journal into her mostly empty backpack. It disappeared into the cavernous sack.

Chapter two

Two hours later, Penny sat at the far corner of a table in the far corner of the cafeteria. Nobody filled the remaining seats; she sat alone. After the absolutely rotten poetry class, Penny was in a foul mood. She ignored the crudités she'd brought for lunch and chewed on the inside of her cheek instead, deep in thought.

Crudités: a fancy and French word for raw vegetables cut up and then arranged on a plate in a design to make them look valuable (the arrangement wasn't essential; they were still crudités if they came packaged in a Tupperware or plastic baggie). Penny preferred her raw vegetables with a side of ranch. Actually, she preferred her ranch with a side of raw vegetables. Once, she and Otis had whipped up a homemade batch of the dressing. It was one of their few concoctions that paled in comparison to the store brand.

Today, Penny brought a wide selection of crudi-tés: uniformly cut bites of carrots, celery, bell pep-pers, string beans, and then (just to shake things up and because they were basically the same size), mini corn straight out of the can. Penny was an efficient vegetable chopper thanks to Otis, who taught her how to properly use a knife.

The air in the cafeteria was warmer than warm. Stifling, practically. The thing about North Georgia: Usually everything was over air-conditioned until at least November. The thing about Lullwater Middle School: Half of the buildings were old, with equally old pipes. Somehow that also meant that the AC petered out halfway through the morning. Penny ran hot, anyway, which she'd always considered a curious trait in someone so small for her age. *Ghost pepper*, Otis called her. One of the hottest chilis out there. Penny fanned herself with her hand, but it didn't help. She craved an ice bath.

Another thing Otis taught her: If you are to blanch vegetables (aka throw them in a pot of furi-ously boiling water for just a couple minutes so the outside cooks a bit but the inside remains crisp), it's necessary to throw them in an ice bath (a big bowl of ice water) afterward to stop the cooking process.

Penny shook herself out of her memory state. Enough about Otis. Now that he was gone, she had to make some friends her own age. That much was apparent. Perhaps it was no coincidence that the corner seat at the corner table she'd sat in almost every lunch since the start of seventh grade afforded her a wide view of the cafeteria action.

Penny had always been a bit of a floater. She wasn't tied down to any specific clique, no stressful obligations of loyalty. She'd never minded not having a group; she'd always had Otis and her lizards at home to keep her company. But with Otis gone, and the lizards nonverbal as ever, Penny was starting to think that maybe there was more to middle school than her self-proclaimed floater status. Maybe having a few companions wouldn't be so bad after all. Problem was, not even three weeks into seventh grade and everything seemed settled. Cliques had formed, groups adhered with invisible glue stickier than toffee.

Cooking relaxed Penny. It was predictable, like math and science, and, better than math and science, if you got your equation right, a reward awaited on the other end in the form of a sweet or savory treat. If you followed the recipe, you knew what you were going to get. Penny had searched far and wide, but could find no recipe for seventh-grade success. All of her initial friend-making attempts fell flat, like skillet cornbread made with expired baking powder. And it wasn't like Penny hadn't tried. Oh, she'd tried.

Friend-making attempt step one: Penny approached the sporty girls first. The volleyball girls and the basketball girls were a bit too tall, so Penny figured she'd ease her way in, starting with the soccer crew. Sports kids seemed like a good target; they'd know all about teamwork and general companionship. It seemed most of the soccer girls played for a team called the Belleayre Fire. They wore their team jackets to school even when it was too hot for a tank top. Penny spent some time on the internet the night before, researching soccer things. That was literally what she'd typed into Google: "Soccer things to talk about."

"Excited for the World Cup?" She'd marched right up to the girl with the red hair but no freckles. Penny didn't know her name. She stood in a triangle with Reem and Shaylah. Or Shaylah and Reem. Penny could not remember who was who, though they didn't look anything alike (Reem was a frizzy-haired brunette with dramatic eyelashes, and Shaylah's tresses hung in a limp blond ponytail, exposing a galaxy of light brown freckles across her nose and cheeks). The three soccer girls all stood in the hallway with soccer bags slung over one shoulder, backpacks over the other.

"Um, the World Cup is in like three years, but sure," Red Hair, No Freckles answered. Reem and Shaylah (or Shaylah and Reem) giggled.

"Well, it's going to be a good one. Anyway, how's the pitch? Not too slippery for your boots?"

Pitch: another word for field. Boots: another word for cleats. Penny's search had yielded some very sport-specific vocabulary.

Reem and Shaylah (or Shaylah and Reem) furrowed their respective brows. Red Hair, No Freckles (what was her name?!) adjusted the strap on her shoulder, but said nothing. Penny felt a telltale tingle in her nose, but she persevered.

"Me, I'd prefer to play division-one soccer before going pro right away. I mean, it would be cool to live in Europe and all." Penny didn't mention that the reason it would be cool to live in Europe was that she could get hands-on culinary training abroad. "But I think that the university system prepares young athletes well," Penny said, as if she knew exactly what young athletes needed to thrive. Penny had memorized that last part.

"I just want to make varsity," Reem or Shaylah said, as if it were an apology.

"You will," the other assured.

"For sure," Penny agreed.

When they turned to go a moment later, presumably to practice, Penny waved goodbye, but couldn't remember any of the other "soccer things to talk about," so she kept her mouth shut. They'd left before she even had a chance to sneeze.

Sure, Penny appreciated a good sprint and a buzzer shot to win the championship, but she was no athlete, at least not in the physical sense. Next.

Friend-making attempt step two: With sports out of the equation, Penny turned her attention to the Gang of Compounding Scientists. Their words, not hers. They'd posted a flyer saying the inaugural Gang of Compounding Scientists meeting would be later that week at lunch. Scientists seemed like a sure bet.

After all, cooking was basically science. Penny planned to tell them that at the first meeting.

But when Penny saddled up to join the four members, science seemed to be the last thing on anybody's mind.

Against all odds, there were two sets of identical twins at Lullwater Middle School. Samson and Sullivan Porter and Jane and Janiyah Jenuzzi. Samson and Sullivan had different haircuts, but the girls were absolutely impossible to tell apart. The quad, which hung out incessantly, was the founding and only members of the Gang of Compounding Scientists, as it turned out.

Penny approached their lunch table and asked, "Gang of Compounding Scientists here?" Two pairs of matching faces looked up and nodded. "New member, reporting for duty."

Penny made a peace sign with her right hand, because at the time, that seemed right. They didn't make room for Penny to sit, so she stood. That was fine. She spent all day sitting at a dumb desk anyway.

"So I was thinking I'd be a great addition to your club, or gang," Penny corrected. Shoot, she'd messed up already. Spark, spark, tingle. She'd planned on explaining herself by saying something like, "Because I'm very experienced in what some consider the ancient art of baking. I know a thing or two about emulsification, too." But the more her nose sparked and tingled, the less confident she felt about her intro speech.

"Actually, we're not doing club stuff. We're in the middle of Fantasy Dream House," Sampson said. That didn't sound very scientific to Penny. It actually sounded the exact opposite of scientific, but she figured she'd play along.

Penny brushed her bangs out of her eyes and said, "Cool."

"You can sit down," one of the girl twins offered, without actually moving to make room.

"S'all good," Penny answered, though her feet were beginning to hurt. That was okay. She needed to toughen them up anyway. Professional cooks had to spend hours on their feet at a time.

"Room made out of diamonds that smells like cotton candy body spray and tastes like campfire marshmallows," one of the girl twins declared.

"Anti-gravity room. Duh," the other girl twin piggybacked.

"Sure, sure," Sampson said in agreement.

"Room just for parakeets," Sullivan added.

"That's so sweet," Penny couldn't help but exclaim.

Sullivan looked at her like his Fantasy Dream House contribution was obvious. Penny's shoulders drooped a bit. A handful of sparks and tingles pinged around in her nose. She shifted her weight to her right foot to give her left leg a rest.

"Your turn, Sulls," Parakeet Twin said.

"After much thought, I must confess that my fantasy dream house would not be complete without a room made entirely of sheepskin-covered trampolines. Because, you know, trampoline burn."

"So obvious."

"Obvious, but necessary," Sullivan said, without missing a beat.

Then they all looked at Penny. It was her turn. Her audition, really.

Though Penny had never officially played Fantasy Dream House, she was pretty sure she understood the rules. "My fantasy dream house will have a room with a cool kitchen? Does that work?" What Penny meant was a kitchen that was actually just a big pantry with all sorts of high-tech equipment like a cast-iron waffle maker, a mandolin slicer, an immersion blender, stand mixer, ice cream maker, one of those laser thermometers that tells the temperature of the thing you point it at . . . the list was basically endless.

"Don't ask me. Your fantasy dream house, your rules," one of the boy twins said matter-of-factly. Something about the way he said it made Penny's stomach feel like applesauce. Without an additional spark or tingle as warning, Penny sneezed.

"Bless you," Jane and Janiyah said at the same time. The boy twins both wiped their hands on their pants, even though they were not the ones who sneezed.

When lunch ended, the Gang of Compounding Scientists dispersed. Penny saw them eating together the next day, but she couldn't tell if it was an official meeting. She was too nervous to go up and ask, so she slunk to the only empty table, the one in the far corner of the cafeteria, and settled into the seat closest to the wall.

Penny ate at the corner table, alone, every day since.

So there Penny sat, watching the soccer girls and

the Gang of Compounding Scientists, along with basically every other kid, nosh on chicken fingers. In that moment, her treasured crudités felt lifeless and inadequate. All of her classmates just raved about the quality of chicken fingers served in the Lullwater cafeteria. Penny was no fool; she loved chicken fingers just as much as the next kid, but she didn't mess with the ones from the cafeteria. She could—and had—made better.

Penny wondered what had gone wrong in her friend-making attempts. Was she unlikable? Penny didn't believe that. Otis always said she was the coolest person six years younger than him that he knew. How was everyone nailing it except for her? She just needed a way to figure out what bonded these other kids together, what they liked, disliked, etc. What they were thinking. Then she'd have a leg up.

Penny's eyes finally settled on Gianna's table, as if it were a magnet. That was often where her gaze landed. Gianna and her best friends, Nayeli and Rose, sat at the table in the center of the room. Not within eavesdropping distance (that would have been exciting!), but certainly at a safe distance to observe. Gianna, Nayeli, and Rose were three of the more fascinating seventh graders at Lullwater Middle School, but Gianna, in particular, interested her most of all.

Which brought Penny to her next friend-making attempt (yet to be executed): Gianna King, the gateway friend.

Everyone loved Gianna. She was the most popular girl in school, and unlike every teen movie ever written, it wasn't because she was a mean girl whom everybody feared. Nope. Gianna wasn't just nice. She was the *nicest*.

What was also crazy was that Gianna was brandnew. "Hot out of Atlanta," she joked when asked. Apparently Gianna had moved to Lullwater at the beginning of the summer. She must have met Rose and Nayeli at the pool or something. That was the only way to explain how just two weeks into seventh grade she already had not one but two best friends.

Gianna King was the type who gave *everybody* a valentine. She smiled at you first. When you gave her a compliment on her shoes or her jacket, she told you where she'd bought them without you having to ask. She always shared the candy she bought from the vending machine. Gianna wanted to be an actress when she grew up. Not film, but Broadway. She didn't need braces; her teeth were perfectly imperfect, the front one on the right ever so slightly angled out. She was so friendly, chatting with anyone and everyone, cheeks always slightly flushed, a charismatic spring in her step. Rumor had it she gave great hugs. Not that Penny knew. She'd never had the good fortune to receive a famous Gianna King hug. Yes, Gianna King was the kind of seventh grader who couldn't make a mistake if she tried. Confident, calm, collected, and perfect.

Gianna King was the gateway friend Penny needed. If she could make friends with Gianna, the rest of the kids at Lullwater Middle School would be eating out of the palm of her hand, literally—once they were officially friends, Penny planned on presenting Gianna with three dozen of her famous Peanut Lover Butter cookies to share with anyone and everyone.

Penny sighed and packed up the remains of her lunch. Three more hours left of school. She could make it, right? She hadn't talked to Otis in several days and was curious to hear about his last few shifts. He'd started a.m. prep (the morning shift where he cut up a gazillion vegetables, measured tons of ingre-dients for dinner recipes, and washed the occasional dish), but quickly moved up to p.m. prep (same thing, but his shift began at 3:00 p.m. instead of 7:00 a.m.). Penny planned to text him from the magnolia tree in her backyard the second she arrived home.

Just then, Penny smelled a deliciously fresh hair product she couldn't place. She glanced up and saw Gianna walking by. Her lips were lightly glossed, her dark hair just shiny enough. She looked straight ahead, backpack resting evenly on her shoulders.

Without the slightest warning, Penny sneezed so hard she feared ranch dressed might come out of her nose. When Penny looked up, expecting to see a dis-gusted look on Gianna's face, instead, to her astonish-ment, Gianna didn't so much as glance in Penny's direction. She proceeded forward, undisturbed.

Gianna's indifference burned. A sizzling drop of oil springing up from a fire-hot skillet. Tiny as a car-bonation bubble, but searing nonetheless.

Chapter three

That evening, Penny sat in the magnolia tree on the branch that looked like a bat wing. The branch hung ten feet above the ground, but Penny could have climbed up blindfolded. It was the one place on earth Penny Hoppe knew by heart.

She was on break. Self-induced break. A pot of Everything-but-Meat Vegetable Soup (Otis's name, not hers) simmered on the stove and one-drop biscuits cooked in the oven. Dinner for four: Mom, Dad, Sylvia (Penny's step-grandma who insisted she be called by her first name), and, of course, Penny. With Otis gone, Penny took it upon herself to cook dinner for her family as often as possible. She faced no challengers for the position. Sylvia refused to do anything more exerting than a crossword puzzle once the sun had set, and Penny's parents worked a lot. Like, *a lot*.

The Hoppes lived in Lullwater, a resort town that

never quite took off. That's how Mom put it. Nestled right between a smattering of North Georgia lakes and the foothills of the Blue Ridge Mountains, it wasn't quite close enough to either attraction to be convenient. It was, however, extremely well placed for the heating and air-conditioning business her parents started four years ago, O&P Temperatures.

"Think about it," they'd said. "Mountain houses need heat, and lake houses need AC."

They weren't wrong, Penny supposed. Because they were still a small, family-run business, after all (Dad's words, not hers), and it was amazing how temperature emergencies, routed directly to Mom's cell phone, came at all hours of the day and night (Mom's words, not hers). Dad often returned home hours after dark, only to leave again at dawn, and Mom was often on the phone fielding service requests.

They'd moved into the little house on Plum Street from an apartment complex across town when Penny was eight. It was the first place they'd lived where they had their own stand-alone mailbox. Penny spent hours staring out the window waiting for the mailman to come. After throwing a mini tantrum about never receiving any mail of her own, Otis occasionally left her notes with imaginary return addresses. She'd saved every one.

Penny looked at the timer on her phone. Twelve more minutes on the biscuits. Penny loved making a family meal (also what restaurants served their staff at the beginning of a shift). It suited her just fine. Better than fine, really. It was great practice: She could test out all the recipes she wanted because Mom, Dad, and Sylvia were not picky eaters. She closed her eyes and inhaled, savoring the damp, mossy air that rushed through her nose and into her lungs. Her short legs dangled on either side of the bat wing–shaped branch.

Speaking of love, Penny also adored the magnolia tree in their backyard. It felt like a private kingdom. This particular magnolia was very tall. "At least a gazillion years old," Otis had told her. Yes, magnolia trees were special, but the magnolia tree in the Hoppes' backyard was especially magnificent.

The tree towered at sixty feet tall. Penny had climbed to the top only once, before realizing that she'd still have to get back down. The magnolia tree was best at night, though. That was when it felt the most private. From Penny's perspective on the bat wing–shaped branch, the leaves were so thick she could neither see nor feel the world outside. She shared the canopied space only with the fireflies persistent enough to penetrate. The inside of the magnolia was a universe and the twinkling bugs were the stars. Magic. She and Otis had spent hours in that tree, talking, laughing, and sometimes in silence, the sigh of the breeze through the leaves the only semblance of chatter.

Penny took out her phone. Otis was probably in the middle of a shift, but sometimes she'd be able to catch him when there was a lull in the restaurant.

Your veg soup and 1 drop biscuits Tonight. Jealous?

Otis replied right away. Vitamix to my right stand mixer to my left. Jealous, ghost pepp?

Otis loved to brag about the fancy equipment in the kitchen of the fancy restaurant where he worked. Aujourd'hui, the spot was called. One of the finest restaurants in Atlanta. Penny had never been. According to Otis, it was stuffy, stuffy, stuffy, but great for his résumé. Plus, he might as well learn the basics from the best.

On his first day, he'd sent her pictures of the

commercial kitchen. Penny stared at the photos time and time again. The giant walk-in freezer, the size of her bedroom, packed with cuts of meat she'd never heard of. The floating metal shelves in the prep space lined with gigantic containers of flour, dried beans, and sugar. And all the tools: dozens of sauté pans hanging from hooks, rows of Vitamixes (the most powerful blender ever), stoves with burners the strength of bonfires. But the coolest part was the open kitchen. Unlike a lot of restaurants, at Aujourd'hui there was no division between the part of the restaurant where people ate and the kitchen where the food was cooked. Customers could actually watch the line cooks juggle multiple orders and plate the dishes.

V jeal, Penny typed back. Then, Any luck on PBttB?

Otis suggested Project Better than the Box the day he revealed he'd gotten a job and would be moving a few days later. Penny was inconsolable. She locked herself in her room and refused to come out until her eyes had dried and her face de-puffed. Penny was not a fan of public crying. And yes, even family members counted as part of the public when it came to crying. When Penny finally emerged, toughest expression she could muster glued to her face, Otis presented her with a stack of pancakes (it was Saturday morning after all) and a challenge.

Neither Penny nor Otis Hoppe were ones to shy away from a challenge. Especially when a recipe was involved.

Project Better than the Box: Invent a recipe for yellow cake that's more delicious than the kind that's made from the box. Despite both Otis and Penny's appreciation for all dishes made from scratch, neither sibling loved anything quite as much as processed cakes. Their absolute, hands-down favorite was yellow cake made from the box, the kind where you just mix in eggs, oil, and water. Over time they'd made that cake at all special occasions, which, in the twelve years Penny had been alive, were mostly birthdays. Not all, but mostly.

The project sounded simple, but easier said than done. With cake, despite the finite amount of ingredients, there were still a considerable number of variables. Flour, sugar, eggs, butter, milk, baking soda, and vanilla could be combined in so many ways. What kind of flour—all-purpose, cake, or some combination? Room-temperature eggs or eggs right from the fridge? Butter high in fat (the French way), or regular unsalted? In the two weeks since Otis had moved, she'd tried two different variations. Both were good, but not great. Neither were better than the box.

Penny wanted to win the challenge—beating her *professional* cook of a big brother was not a title she took lightly. In the back of her mind, though, she dreaded the day either of them emerged as victors. Their competition reminded Penny that they were still connected, even if they were two hours, two roofs, and seemingly two worlds away. Once the project was over, the invisible cord would be cut.

Penny's nose tingled, then sparked, then tingled again.

She let her phone screen lock to black. She took another deep breath and watched the fireflies. She liked how they never blinked in the same spot twice.

Four minutes later, her timer went off. Otis still hadn't responded, so Penny issued a taunt.

Don't think you have a leg up cuz of the stand mixer. Ghost pepp never loses!

And then, a request.

Also when u think we can come to the resto?

With that, Penny shoved her phone into her back pocket, scrambled out of the magnolia tree, and trotted into the house to retrieve her biscuits out of the oven.

After the soup-and-biscuit dinner, everyone assumed position. Dad snored on the couch in front of the fish tank full of free-range lizards (his description, not hers).

A few years ago, he came home with a fish tank he'd gotten on sale. They'd filled it with neon goldfish, but the filter proved too powerful and sucked the poor dudes right up within a week. Not willing to risk another goldfish casualty, he turned the tank into a lizard box, filled only with little lizards they'd found in the yard or at clients' houses. Dad had cut out TV for his New Year's resolution, so after dinner he watched the lizards instead. They didn't move much, and he always fell asleep within minutes. Mom retreated upstairs, headset still in, customer servicing in her pajamas.

Only Sylvia and Penny remained at the kitchen table. Penny carefully looked over Sylvia's shoulder at her crossword puzzle. Key word, *carefully.* Sylvia was one part ladybug, one part summer breeze, and one part snapping turtle. Sylvia's words, not Penny's. Every clue was crossed off except for one.

"Forty-six across just might kill me," Sylvia said, not taking her eyes off the paper. Sylvia did a crossword every day, "To keep my mind sharper than yours," she said. *Yours* referring to anyone and everyone.

"Doubt it," Penny replied. Penny knew Sylvia well enough to know that saying anything that indicated you didn't want Sylvia around was a big mistake.

"Ha, no six-letter word can take me down." Sylvia punched her right fist in the air.

"Didn't think so," Penny confirmed. "Want me to look up the answer on my phone?"

"Don't be a fool," Sylvia shot back. Penny smiled; she liked Sylvia's sharp tongue. They went through this routine often.

"We don't cheat around here," the two said together.

"No, we don't cheat," Penny repeated.

"Unless you know who's going to win the horse race. Then, we cheat." There were a few things that Sylvia loved. Betting on horses, crossword puzzles, and romance novels. Sylvia was truly like nobody Penny had ever met.

Penny stood and went to preheat the oven to 350

degrees. She wanted to take another stab at Project Better than the Box before bed. It was Friday night after all; why not go a little wild?

As Penny began taking ingredients out of the pantry, she said, "Last go was a little too spongy, so I'm thinking less b-powder." When the spirit moved her, she liked to narrate her process. Though Sylvia rarely responded, she still felt like a worthy audience. Penny measured out the dry ingredients into a mixing bowl.

"Mhm," Sylvia said, hunched over her puzzle.

"And I stand by my decision that room-temperature eggs just make more sense. But to double-confirm I'll use two right out of the fridge today."

"Mhmmm."

"Two eggs didn't provide the body I'd hoped for, but I'm thinking that's because I used the hand mixer. I'll use a whisk this time. You can't overbeat eggs and expect success. Right, Sylvia?"

"Mhmmm."

"We'll taste-test this one together, okay?" Sylvia usually provided Penny's first taste test for a new recipe. Mostly due to proximity rather than interest.

"Mhmmm."

"I'm also going to add some bacon, applesauce, and a lizard tail. Sound good?"

"Mhmmm. Bake away, Ghost Pepper."

Fifty-five minutes later Penny carefully took the cake out of the oven. The two major Project Better than the Box rules were that you had to finish eating one cake before starting a next (wasteful is distasteful, Otis said) and no taste-testing with icing. Once the cake had slightly cooled, Penny cut two small squares: one for her and one for Sylvia.

"What do you think?" Penny asked after a few chews.

"Needs icing, if you ask me."

"Sylvia, you know taste-testing with icing is cheating. Crowds the palate."

"I don't cheat!" Sylvia declared.

The cake was mediocre. Average. Not better than the box. Quite a bit worse than the box, in actuality. Penny lay in bed that night mulling it over. *Probably an egg issue*, she thought. Or it could be a temperature-of-the-oven issue. Or a not-enough-vanilla-extract issue. Maybe she needed a stand mixer or some tool she just didn't have, or worse, didn't even know existed. Lots of potential issues. The variables sifted through Penny's brain as her mind started to fog with sleep.

Penny checked her phone one last time before rolling onto her side. No text back from Otis. Dinner service must have been busy. No Project Better than the Box news to report, anyway. She hadn't discovered the recipe. Not just yet.

Chapter Four

"Penny girl, take a ride with me."

Penny looked up from her phone. She'd spent the rainy Saturday morning lounging on the couch, perusing recipes online. Apparently she'd been doing that for hours. She could really get lost down that rabbit hole.

"Where?"

"Tina's." Tina, Mom's BFF since their Friday Night Skate days (whatever that meant), owned and operated a thrift store a few towns over. At the start of every season, she ran a clothing drive. Four times a year Mollie Hoppe used her client service skills for a good cause; *O&P Temperatures will pick up and drop off*, meaning Mollie Hoppe accepted bags of donated clothes from their residential clients and brought them, on her own time, to Tina's Treasures. "We all have an obligation to give back," she said. "Got a record-breaking haul; I'm gonna need some extra hands."

Penny rolled onto her side. Tina's Treasures did have a hit-or-miss used-appliance section where she'd scored a decent mixing bowl once. But it was also a forty-five-minute drive away.

"It's so far," Penny complained. The couch was so comfortable, the outside was so rainy . . .

"Bendy's for breakfast?"

Penny shot upright. "Gimme five."

Bendy's was an ice cream stand in Mason Mill, just down the block from Tina's. Best ice cream on the planet. They also served coffee in the morning, and if you played your cards right, or happened to have a mom who went to high school with Miss Bendy herself, they'd open up the ice cream vault as early as 8:00 a.m. Penny was a big fan of eating foods at untraditional times of day. "Breakfast for dinner" got a lot of attention, but that innovation didn't hold a flame to "dessert for breakfast." Ice cream as a first meal of the day was Penny's favorite decadence.

Penny fiddled with her phone as Mom drove down

the windy back roads. Mom avoided the interstates when she could help it. The scenery was better off the highway. The North Georgia forest sometimes had a mystical quality to it, especially at the tail end of an early morning rain. Through the dense trees, fog dusted the tops of the distant Blue Ridge Mountains.

"So, how was the second week of seventh grade, Penny girl?" Mom asked.

Awful? Embarrassing? Confusing? All of the above?

"It was okay," Penny answered.

"Just okay?"

"Yeah, I mean, same, same, same," Penny deferred. They drove another minute in silence. A cheesy old Heat Squad song played on the radio. Mom hummed along.

"Don't know if I'm awake, you're my dream reality," Mom sang a few notes under pitch.

"Soooo," Penny interrupted. She loved Mom, liked Heat Squad okay, but couldn't really handle the two of them together. "Otis said he'd probably be able to get us a friends-and-family reservation at Aujourd'hui, like, any day now. So maybe we can go soon?" Even though the restaurant booked up months in advance (thanks to a glowing review in *Fine & Dine* magazine), Otis said he'd probably be able to get them a "friends-and-family" reservation *and* discount. Ka-ching! The beginning of truffle season was fast approaching, according to Otis and the internet. Penny had never tried a truffle, the mysterious mushroom that came from Italy and tasted like something called umami, which was an equally mysterious extra taste bud or something. Truffles were impossible to come by in Lullwater, and equally impossible to afford, but Otis said he'd try to hook it up. "By the end of the month, I'm thinking." Penny did the quick math. Twenty days left in September. An eternity, basically.

"Mhmmm," is all Mom said. Penny couldn't tell if Mom was responding to her or humming to the song. A high-pitched teenage boy's voice wafted through the car speakers.

Penny quickly typed out a text to Otis. He was certainly still sleeping at this hour, but he'd see it when he woke up.

Mom's in for f&f end of Sept!

Before Penny could explain all she knew about truffles, Mom's phone rang.

"I swear," she mumbled, working to untangle the wires of her earbuds before the call went to voicemail. "If I had known there'd be so many AC emergencies, I'd have stayed in retail and called it a dang day." Earbuds in, call accepted. "Thank you for calling O&P Temperatures, this is Mollie, how may I help you today?"

Sorry, she mouthed to Penny, but Penny was used to it. She rested her head against the window and drifted off into a windy, bumpy snooze.

"I know you're not bringing that drippy cone into my store," Roxanna called from behind the counter without looking up.

"It's not your store!" Penny shouted from just outside the door. She shoved the last bite of her pistachio-saturated waffle cone into her mouth.

"Mornin', Roxanna," Mom said sweetly as she breezed into the store, giant sack of clothes over her shoulder. "Tina here? I'm gonna make her day."

Roxanna just pointed toward the back.

"Thank you, love." Mom was not fazed by Roxanna.

"You have sprinkles on your cheeks," Roxanna grumbled as Penny shuffled into the store.

"Do not."

"But do you?"

Roxanna was a weirdo. Penny didn't *not* like her. But she also hoped, for Roxanna's sake (and Tina's), she'd find a new job soon. Roxanna had worked the register at Tina's Treasures for as long as Penny could remember, and she seemed to hate every second of it. Penny admired Roxanna for the risks she took with her remarks and with her bangs. Both were severe. Roxanna's resting face could make any new and vulnerable customer run out of the store in tears. Penny wasn't scared of her, though. She was used to hanging out with older kids, all of Otis's friends. Roxanna was vaguely Otis's age, Penny thought.

"Goldfish don't have stomachs," Penny called as she walked to the kitchenware section. She always did her best to throw Roxanna off. It rarely worked, but it was always fun to try.

Penny strolled toward the appliance aisle. She heard Mom and Tina gabbing in the back of the store. Once they got started there was no stopping them;

Penny had ample time to peruse. Much of the inventory in the appliance aisle had been there for ages. Mismatched forks, creaky toasters, a chipped punch bowl; things that looked *almost* functional. But every now and then Penny found a gem, or more aptly put, a treasure.

Penny had her hopes up for one of four items in particular: a stand mixer (possible, but unlikely), a Vitamix (would take a miracle), a slushie machine (not out of the question), and a pour-over coffee maker (Penny didn't drink the stuff yet, but when she started she planned to slurp away in style). As Penny turned into the aisle, she let her fingertips drift over the merchandise jutting off the overstuffed shelves.

The recipe box rested on the end of the bottom shelf, nestled between a rusty skillet and an electric kettle that had maybe never been cleaned. It caught Penny's eye immediately. Penny wouldn't have been able to explain why the box stood out; it wasn't the object's newness alone. It was a simple brown box; the front about the size of an index card, with the word *Recipe* carved on top in precise lettering. Penny leaned over to retrieve the object from the shelf, gently, as if carrying a baby bird to safety. She opened the lid and saw the inside was painted a rich cherry red. Penny flipped through the dozen or so recipe cards inside; rectangles with *Recipe Name*, *Ingredients*, and *Directions* printed on the front. Every card was blank, just waiting to be filled in. She was about to close the lid when something else caught her eye, a glint of silver behind the very last recipe card.

Penny peered closer and found a necklace: a delicate silver chain threaded a key-shaped charm. A small, circular stone sat at the top of the key. Penny examined the stone. An enthralling dark blue, but not quite. It was a color she'd never seen before. What color was it? Not black, not *not* purple. It just felt deep. Like staring into outer space. Penny touched the stone again with the tip of her pinky. It was ice-cold. Instantly, Penny felt refreshed, as if she'd just downed a mint lemonade on the hottest summer day. The only jewelry Penny wore was a pair of small, circular stud earrings and an anklet made of ribbon that just wouldn't fall off. This necklace was the perfect addition that Penny hadn't known she'd needed. Penny couldn't help but feel that this plain yet delicate necklace was meant for her.

"Five minutes, Penny girl," Mom called. "And you

better hold me to it!" Penny heard Mom's and Tina's distant laughs, but all her attention was on her new-found treasure. Penny quickly pulled the necklace out of the box, snapped the lid shut, and marched to the register.

"Neither does a platypus, you know!" Roxanna said once Penny approached. Roxanna stared at Penny and narrowed her eyes.

"What?"

Roxanna pointed to her belly. Penny laughed. Roxanna huffed, but Penny caught the slight twitch of a smile in the corner of her mouth.

"Does this necklace come with the recipe box?" Penny asked. She opened her palm to reveal the charm.

"Does it look like I make the rules?"

"I honestly do not know." Sometimes Penny wished Roxanna would just answer a darn question.

Roxanna searched under the tin for a price sticker. "Secrets Necklace. Twelve dollars."

"No, not just the necklace, the box, too. Also, not a secret."

Roxanna leaned in closer and spoke very slowly. "Does it look like I make the rules?" Penny truly could not tell if Roxanna was doing her a favor or threatening her well-being. It was more hilarious than scary. Roxanna then turned the box over so Penny could see. Sure enough, the sticker on the bottom described the item as *Secrets Necklace*. Odd.

"Okaaay, so twelve for everything? The box, recipe cards, and necklace?"

"You teenyboppers can be so dense," Roxanna said, rolling her eyes.

Penny wasn't sure what a teenybopper was. "I'm in seventh grade, if you're wondering. I think you should know that by now." Penny had been coming to Tina's with her mom since practically the beginning of time.

"Twelve bones. Take it or leave it."

Penny slapped a ten-dollar bill on the counter just as Mom emerged from her gossip session with Tina. Sometimes it was best to play hardball with Roxanna.

"Penny girl, you got to keep me honest. You know I lose track of time back there."

Without another word, Roxanna picked up the ten and pushed the box toward Penny with one finger, as if it were covered in raw eggs, too bacteria-infested to touch. Penny took that as permission to clasp the necklace around her neck.

"Hey, Penny baby!" a voice called from the back office. Tina rarely showed her face on the premises. Part of a necessary mystique, she insisted; whatever that meant.

"Hey, Miss Tina!" Penny shouted back.

"C'mon, let's go, Penny. Dad called about a new service appointment scheduled for two. Yay. Bye, Roxanna, love, see you next time."

"Bye, love you; don't mean it."

Penny gave Roxanna a peace sign, because she thought it looked cool and because in all honesty she thought Roxanna could benefit from some calming vibes.

"Later," Penny added over her shoulder as she walked out the door, recipe box in one hand, necklace around her neck. The rain had finally stopped, yielding radiant sunshine. Steam rose off the asphalt parking lot, and the air was already thick and humid. Penny felt a tingle right below the dip in her collarbones. Unlike Penny Hoppe, the silver necklace with the key-shaped charm ran very, very cold.

Chapter Five

Otis finally texted Penny back late Sunday night. Early Monday morning, technically. When Penny woke up for school, the awaiting message gave her a little jolt.

Crazy weekend. Weeds nonstop. Better be keepin' it weird up in L-WATER for me.

Penny smiled. She loved, just loved, when Otis used kitchen lingo. *Weeds*, or *in the weeds*, meant super, duper, can't-think-straight, maybe-mess-up-an-order busy.

Talking to chef this week. Ask about f&f. Prob 3 weeks. At least.

Penny's smile faded. Three weeks? That was basically forever away.

Why so long? she replied.

It wasn't the three weeks that bothered her. It was the "at least." That sounded like the opposite of promising.

What if I bring my world-famous Peanut Butter Lover cookies?

Penny hoped that would do the trick. Otis was a sucker for anything peanut butter, baked or otherwise. He swore nobody made Peanut Butter Lover cookies as good as Penny.

As the morning continued, Penny wasn't able to shake her rotten mood. The fact that it was Fourth of July weather in mid-September certainly didn't help. It was only 8:05 a.m. and already muggy. Sometimes Penny wished they lived in Chicago. She heard it was cold there. Or better yet, Norway, or the top of Canada. Or maybe they could just summer in the North Pole. Anywhere that wasn't eighty-five degrees with eighty-five percent humidity in mid-September. Penny appreciated a good heat wave or two in May, but these early autumn temperatures were a little much.

Penny wiped her brow and crossed the street toward Lullwater Middle School. Her bangs stuck to her forehead. Bangs were worth it seven months out of the year, just long enough to make her forget about the hottest months when they weren't.

Yes, Penny ran hot. Ghost pepper hot.

The entrance to Lullwater Middle School was wonky and grand. The facade implied academy, not small-town public school. The main building had once been a bank or a train station or some sort of important government building that couldn't be altered or touched for historic landmark reasons. The walls were made of old red brick, and the windows were extra tall with arched tops. Thick columns propped up a sort of overhang, sheltering the area outside the front entrance to the school.

The Cavern, students called it, for reasons to do with dampness and lack of natural light. Before and after school, the Cavern was the place to be. With the exception of the East Hallway, which contained the gym, cafeteria, and a few creaky classrooms, all other structures were brand-new. All this meant, as far as Penny was concerned, was that she had to wait until second-period science, when she had class in the West Wing, for adequate air-conditioning. O&P Temperatures would really have a field day if they could get their hands on that middle school.

Penny was so hot, and so slimy, and the Cavern was so crowded and noisy. Students congregated in claustrophobic clumps, as if savoring their last minutes of non-classroom time. Penny did not understand why it was necessary to socialize in the condensed area when there was plenty of room to spread out along the sidewalk that lead to the Cavern. *Seventh graders*, Penny thought, shaking her head.

Penny stepped into the crowd and felt a tingle in her nose. And then a tingle in the center of her chest, just below the collar of her shirt. That was odd. Penny looked down and remembered her new necklace. Tucked under her light purple tank top, the key shape charm made a slight bump in the spot just above her sternum. The necklace, unlike Penny's body temperature and the surrounding air, maintained a radiant cool, as if it had just been pulled out of the refrigerator. Penny grasped the charm in her hand, and then brought it to her cheek, as if it were an ice cube. Ahhh, that felt nice. Somewhat calmed by the newfound source of chill, Penny waded toward the front doors. If people would just move out of her way, she'd have time to splash some water on her face before class started.

Penny had never noticed just how echoey the Cavern was. Though she knew nobody was actually talking to her, voices, sounding simultaneously distant and near, and from every direction, swirled into her ears. Penny brushed shoulders, bumped the occasional backpack, and absorbed snippets of her classmates' conversations as she made her way through the crowd. Bits of conversations, like stray puzzle pieces, floated in and out of Penny's ears.

T.C. is wearing that same shirt again.
I wish I had toast for breakfast.
Cole won't even look at me.
Shaylah has the best ponytail.
My toe hurts. Dumb shoe choice.
If I close my eyes, maybe nobody can see me.
This will end, this will end.
I should have snoozed my alarm more.
My legs look like rectangles.

The voices all swirled together like an egg just cracked into batter; not yet fully combined, but not separate, either. Penny, thankful for the ice-cube charm in her hand, ignored the trickle of sweat that fell down her back, and pushed her way inside.

Penny knew that Otis wouldn't be up early, but

she couldn't help but check her phone every time a teacher turned their back. This "at least three weeks" thing was not going to cut it. By third period, Penny was pulling her phone out every few minutes.

"Hand it over, Ms. Hoppe." Penny looked up to see Mr. Turney towering over her. His wild nose hairs were on display. Penny quickly looked away and raised her hands like a criminal, dropping her phone in her lap.

"Wasn't me!" she said.

Mr. Turney held out his hand and waited. Reluctantly, Penny shoved her phone into his probably clammy paw.

"Busted," Cole mumbled from the back row.

Penny fiddled with the key-shaped charm around her neck. Already, the jewelry felt like a bit of a security blanket.

In front of her, Mateo tapped his foot on the ground to an inaudible beat. *Tap-tap, tap-tap.* Annoying. Penny was about to ask him to cut it out when she heard him say, "Boogers are my main source of sodium, now that I think about it."

His voice sounded bizarre; echoey. But mostly Penny couldn't believe he'd said that out loud! And in the middle of class! What was he thinking? Penny gazed around the room but nobody else seemed to have heard. How was that possible? Penny looked back at Foot Tapper. He continued to tap away, as if he hadn't just said the most ludicrous thing possible.

Whoa. Just thinking about it made Penny's nose tingle.

"You can retrieve your dear mobile device after school, Ms. Hoppe." With that, Mr. Turney tucked Penny's phone into the bottom drawer of his desk and continued with the lesson on Greek mythology that Penny hadn't been listening to in the first place.

Penny's Monday didn't exactly improve after her third-period cell-phone confiscation. Mrs. Li scolded her for zoning out (she couldn't argue with that), she realized at the start of lunch that she'd actually forgotten her lunch (sitting right there on the kitchen counter—she could just see it), and Cole played some stupid trick to get Reem's attention, which resulted in Penny tripping over his backpack and nearly decapitating herself on the door of a locker (Cole didn't even apologize, though Reem did help her up).

Finally the day was over, and Penny made the necessary detour to Mr. Turney's room. She'd probably have countless messages from Otis by now. Hopefully he wouldn't be mad that she hadn't responded. Nah, Otis could easily imagine what was up; he probably still held the world record for cell-phone confiscations from back in his middle school days.

"Welcome back, Ms. Hoppe. Have thee repented?" Mr. Turney said as Penny walked into his classroom. On the first day of school, Mr. Turney had humble-bragged that he'd spent the summer performing at the Appalachian State renaissance fair. Nobody had been surprised. Or impressed.

"Sure," Penny mumbled, hardly looking up. But then she did, and then she saw her. Gianna stood right at Mr. Turney's desk, cheery as ever.

Penny sneezed immediately.

"Bless you," Gianna said, without actually looking at her. Then, "Thanks, Mr. Turney. Your support of the Thespians Association is much appreciated!"

Penny's cheeks burned. She grabbed her charm in efforts to cool off. Why wouldn't Gianna look at her?

"My pleasure, Ms. King, just let me know what you need. Happy to help," Mr. Turney said from his seat behind the desk.

Gianna smiled again, spun on her heel, and walked out the door.

"I hope people like baked goods," she heard Gianna's voice echo from behind her. If Mr. Turney hadn't interjected, Penny would have confirmed that, yes, anyone with a lick of sense liked a baked good. Weird thing to be concerned about. And Gianna's strange, echoey voice definitely sounded concerned.

"Now, was your day that much worse without your phone?" Mr. Turney asked as he reached down to the bottom drawer of his desk. It seemed to take a surprising amount of effort.

"I know, technology is evil, it's rotting our brains, and I was finally able to smell the daisies or roses or whatever all day long and I'm a better person for it." Penny was in a sassy mood.

Luckily, Mr. Turney did have a sense of humor. Now that the school day was over, he appeared more relaxed. He grinned. "Never short of spunk, Ms. Hoppe. Here you go." He handed her the phone. "Enjoy."

Once in the hallway, Penny checked her texts. Nothing. Not one word from Otis. Not one. Penny, for the billionth time that sticky Monday, pushed her bangs out of her eyes and headed home. There was only one thing that could lift her mood.

Chapter Six

Peanut Butter Lover cookies was the first recipe that Penny felt was her own. The base of the recipe came from an old southern cookbook Otis had found at Tina's, but Penny'd added her own twist. A secret ingredient, if you will. Not even Otis knew what it was. Penny had memorized the recipe—measurements and steps—by heart. She'd made them that many times. As they were baking in the oven after school, only then did Penny remember her new recipe box from Tina's and have the idea to write hers for the cookies down. The recipe box could be her own little space for culinary treasures. It came with all those blank recipe cards; might as well put them to use.

"Don't let the cookies burn," Penny said to Sylvia, as she walked out of the kitchen and to her room, even though Penny would never be reckless enough to let her food burn. Sylvia sat at the kitchen table reading a book titled *Honestly, Jacques* and taking notes in the margins with a red colored pencil.

"Cookies don't burn," she murmured, mind obviously elsewhere.

"Exactly," Penny said with a chuckle as she trotted to her bedroom. Baking the cookies had put her in a better mood already. By the time the dinner Penny planned to make was in the oven—a simple but effective turkey-and-spinach lasagna—Penny hoped her Monday funk would be long expired.

Penny had left the recipe box on her nightstand. Traditionally, a recipe box belonged in the kitchen, but Penny didn't want to share anything about her new treasure. Not even the sight of it. She knew that was a little selfish, but Penny didn't mind.

Penny didn't consider herself a forgetful person. She knew countless recipes by heart, both simple (marinara sauce, lasagna, meat loaf) and more complex (sweet corn chowder, waffle batter, dulce de leche). She'd have pasta cooking on the stove, veggies roasting in the oven, and be making a salad dressing on the counter all at the same time, never forgetting to drain the penne or remove the carrots from the broiler. So when Penny opened the recipe box, she was shocked. Both with what she saw and the fact that she hadn't noticed it before.

The first card, right at the front of the stack, read *Recipe Name: The Secrets Necklace.* Below, written out as if it were a recipe for pie or roast chicken or macaroni and cheese or any actual meal, were the ingredients and instructions.

Penny truly remembered that all the recipe cards had been blank when she first gazed inside the box at Tina's Treasures. Maybe she'd overlooked one? Certainly not the one in the front, though. Maybe they'd gotten shuffled during transport? Seemed unlikely; Penny wasn't reckless with her belongings. The overhead fluorescent light at Tina's was a little hazy, now that Penny thought about it. Still, Penny was not a forgetful person, and a recipe for a *necklace* of all things was not something she'd have overlooked.

Strange. Very, very strange.

Penny carefully removed the completed recipe card from the bright red interior of the box, and sat on her bed cross-legged. She kept very still as she read, fearful that with any sudden movement the writing would blow away like grains of salt in the wind.

RECIPE NAME: THE SECRETS NECKLACE

Ingredients:
1. Secrets Necklace (chain, key-shaped charm)
2. Your neck (duh, it's a necklace)

Directions:

Oven temperature: Ghost Pepper hot

Cook Time: As long as necessary (your Secrets Necklace will be the judge of that)

Step 1: Wear your new Secrets Necklace around your neck. It's okay if it shows; it is beautiful, after all.

Step 2: Get within eavesdropping distance of a *peer*. Eavesdropping distance is a bit different for everybody, so a good way to judge is if you can hear them talking, silly.

Step 3: Hold the charm on your Secrets Necklace in your hand. If you're hot, which you might be, you can touch it to your cheek (as you may have already noticed, your Secrets Necklace runs cold). That will feel nice, but not enhance the powers of the necklace in any way.

Step 4: While holding your necklace, place your attention on whose thoughts you wish to hear.

Step 5: Listen. The echo means it's working.

Fine Print: This necklace is not effective on grown-ups or animals (don't worry, pet lizards are not offended). For best results, do not substitute any of the ingredients or modify the steps in any way. And don't forget—keep it weird!

Penny read the recipe again. And then again. She took a walk around her room, splashed some water on her face, and then read the recipe a third time. She thought about texting Otis, but hesitated. Though the instructions didn't mention anything about it, Penny was certain that the Secrets Necklace information was meant for her and her alone.

Penny thought back through her day. All the

echoey voices she'd heard in the Cavern before school, Mateo's bizarre comment during class, and her brief non-interaction with Gianna in Mr. Turney's room. Was it possible? Could the necklace that hung around her neck, that already felt like a permanent part of her body, allow her to hear the thoughts of those around her? That would be . . .

Penny wasn't sure what it would be. Scary. Right? What would it mean to know people's secrets? Penny reflected on the first two weeks of seventh grade. She thought about all the times she'd felt stupid around the boys in her grade, self-conscious around the girls, and vice versa. And the sneezing. There'd been a lot of sneezing. Way too much sneezing. Everything about seventh grade was so embarrassing mainly because it was so confusing. Maybe, just maybe, this Secrets Necklace—if it worked like the recipe promised—could clear things up.

Whoa.

"Cookies are doin' something," Sylvia screeched from the other room. Sylvia's articulation couldn't be counted on when she was in the middle of one of her books. Penny quickly put the recipe card back in the recipe box, shoved the container under her bed just in case (in case of what?), and rushed into the kitchen. Her phone lay on the counter, timer beeping. "Timer," Sylvia said calmly as Penny arrived.

"How long has it been going off?" Penny asked, still a little rattled.

"Who knows? Thirty seconds, thirty hours? Don't expect me to pay attention when Jacques is in the picture." Sylvia gave her book a little shake and wiggled her eyebrows

"Gross, Sylvia," Penny said, but Sylvia offered no indication she'd heard.

Penny pulled the cookies out of the oven, just in time. The edges were golden and crisp, and the centers puffed up with just the right amount of air. They were perfect.

Little-known fact: Nutmeg, fresh grated nutmeg, really put the "peanut" in "peanut butter." That was the secret ingredient. Penny'd discovered it by mistake, and had never made a batch without the spice since.

Penny hardly spoke at dinner that night. When Mom complimented her on the lasagna, Penny just nodded, sacrificing the opportunity to explain that she'd browned the turkey with an extra clove of garlic this time. When Mom retreated to the bedroom, Penny joined Dad on the couch. She wasn't quite ready to be alone. Together, they watched the lizards.

Millions, Scraffy, and Rent were their names. Penny had named Millions, Otis claimed Scraffy's namesake, and Sylvia was responsible for Rent. "Because that's what he oughta be paying." Sylvia cackled at her own jokes. No, Millions, Scraffy, and Rent didn't do much, but at times like this they were nice to have around. Three extra heartbeats under their roof was the way Penny thought about it. Seven heartbeats instead of eight sounded heartier than four heartbeats instead of five.

"Penny for your thoughts," Dad said after a few minutes.

"I wouldn't have let you name me Penny if I'd known that's what you'd say to me every day."

"Dollar for your thoughts, then," Dad countered.

"Two. In the form of a two-dollar bill." Otis always kept a two-dollar bill in his wallet for good luck.

"Deal." Dad mimed pulling his wallet out of his back pocket and slapping an invisible two-dollar bill into Penny's open palm. Penny giggled. This act was familiar.

"Otis said someone hid raw eggs in the grill cook's apron the other night," Penny said, recounting the text she'd received earlier that evening. "He was so close to the grill that one of them cooked a little. The other ones . . . well, you can imagine."

Dad chuckled, but said nothing more. They settled into another easy silence. Millions joined Scraffy on a twig. The two perched together, waiting. For something. Rent lay in the opposite corner. It was unclear if Rent was watching Millions and Scraffy or if it was the other way around. Maybe they were all watching each other. Lizard stare-off.

"What's going on in that head of yours, Penny girl?" Dad asked, breaking his daughter out of her reptilian daydream.

Penny thought about how to answer. In short, a lot.

"Do you think they're pals?" Penny asked, pointing to the three lizards in the tank.

"I hope so."

"Me too," Penny said, without realizing those were the words that were going to come out.

"Even lizards need pals."

"Even lizards need pals," Penny repeated.

She fell asleep watching her pets that night, only to awake hours later, clammy, hot, and nearly suctioned to the pleather couch. Something had woken her up, but like a dream slipping away into the fog of sleep, Penny couldn't quite figure out what. When Penny tucked into her bed, toes poking out the bottom of her thin sheet, she felt the chill from her necklace through her shirt. Drowsily, only half awake, Penny closed her right hand over the charm and nestled deeper into her pillow. She fell back asleep immediately.

That night, Penny dreamed she was Millions on his first day of skydiving school.

Chapter Seven

First order of Secrets Necklace business: a slow lap around the cafeteria. That really seemed like the best way. Such a stroll would grant Penny maximum eavesdropping access. Besides, when else would so many of her peers be stationary, congregated, and least likely to notice a four-foot-eight-inch-tall girl with thick blond bangs prowling from table to table? Penny was excited to put her Secrets Necklace to the test.

She wouldn't look anyone in the eye—that seemed a little too suspicious, not to mention bizarre in light of her crawling pace. Penny preferred to listen in without being noticed—incognito mode. Anyway, nowhere in the Secrets Necklace recipe did it say she needed to make eye contact in order to effectively eavesdrop.

It was green bean day. Aka the worst-smelling

day of the week. Penny half expected her slow lap to yield the same sentiment over and over: *Why do green beans smell like farts?* She identified the scent of the unimpressive vegetable before she even entered the cafeteria. From the outside, Penny saw lunch was in full swing. Most tables were occupied and voices, whoops, and some laughter blended together like a smoothie. Penny took one step toward the cafeteria entrance and sneezed, but she didn't turn back. Penny clasped her hand around the ever-cool key-shaped charm. "Secrets Necklace slow-lap lunch, here I come," she whispered to herself.

Penny had planned ahead: She'd consumed an extra-big breakfast so she wouldn't need to actually eat during lunch. Still, she got in the food line. Penny'd seen enough syndicated detective shows (Sylvia's fourth-favorite pastime) to know that she couldn't just slow-lap empty handed—that would be suspicious and peculiar, and possibly hurricane-level sneeze inducing. She couldn't risk it. Penny needed at least an apple juice in one hand to convincingly appear like she was searching for a place to sit, not telepathically snooping on all of her classmates.

Mateo and an eighth-grade girl Penny didn't know

stood in front of her. Mateo was being, well, not Mateo-ish at all. That's to say, uncharacteristically quiet. Penny brought her left hand to the key-shaped charm around her neck, focused her attention on the duo, and listened.

"So then we had to turn the car around because we were totally going the wrong way," the girl said.

Mateo nodded vigorously in response. Penny then heard him think, *Don't say a word. If my voice cracks, she'll know all about my puberty.*

"Which was such a waste of time because it was already, like, late in the afternoon," the girl said, before thinking, *Mateo is such a good listener!*

"Mhmmm," Mateo murmured, before thinking, *Puberty is so embarrassing.*

"And we wanted to get to the lighthouse by sunset. For selfies, obviously." *I'll show him a selfie, but only if he asks.*

Mateo made a face that implied, *Of course*, though he thought, *Life is so embarrassing.*

"But then my phone died . . ." *My phone's not dead now . . .*

Another silent Mateo nod as he thought, *If my voice cracks, she'll hate me.*

"And we were like five minutes too late for sunset, anyways," the girl complained, then thought, *Please ask to see a selfie, please, please.*

"Mhmmm." *And if she hates me, then I'll just die. So don't talk. Don't talk.*

"And I guess that's why I don't do the Gulf of Mexico anymore."

Before Penny had time to listen to another of the girl's thoughts, Mateo said, "I have to go!" As he sped away, Penny heard him think, *Why did I do that, why did I do that, everything is so horrible and embarrassing.*

He hates me, the girl thought.

Oof. That was brutal. Penny had no idea cracking voices was such a preoccupation for seventh-grade dudes.

Finally, Penny had an apple juice in hand, and was ready to go. She cruised by the table where the theater kids sat first.

I'm so bad at mask work, Penny heard first.

If I don't get a lead in the spring musical, I'll die.

Stella Adler and Stanislavski are basically the same, right?

Penny remembered the time she'd tried to sit with

them, and how confused she'd been by all their talk of various acting techniques. Turns out, she wasn't alone.

At the next table, Penny heard a boy wearing hiking boots think, *I'm not cool enough to sit with them*, clearly referring to the theater kids. When Penny sneaked a glance to match a face with the thought, her eyes landed on a dude surrounded by three girls obviously vying for his attention.

Hiking Boots Romeo looks pretty cool to me, Penny thought to herself.

Half a lap later, she approached Cole's table. Penny nearly turned around. No doubt Cole's inner monologue would only reveal mean jokes and crude comments. Penny wasn't sure she wanted to know any of that. But before she could make a decision, she was well within the eavesdropping bubble of his table. Cole sat across from two girls from their homeroom. Their conversation faded into background noise, and their echoey thoughts moved to the forefront, sounding the way a distant mirage on a desert highway might look.

Why won't Cole talk to me?

Why won't Cole stop talking to me?

I bet if I flex my muscles, my armpit hair will grow longer. And faster. Yeah! Do it, Cole.

Sure enough, Cole flexed. One girl giggled, and the other rolled her eyes.

Next were the Gang of Compounding Scientists. Penny saw that they all examined a single printout of the periodic table. Penny held her charm tight and watched the group.

"So can we all commit to memorizing the chart by next week?" Samson asked. Penny noticed he tapped his toe on the ground, as if communicating in Morse code.

The other members of the crew murmured in agreement.

I should tell Jane, Penny heard a girl twin think. *What's the big deal, right? We've had crushes before. Who cares if mine is on Samson. Right? Right. But really, right?*

Penny shifted her attention to Jane and heard, *Samson is so bossy.*

So Janiyah had a crush on Samson, and now Penny knew the difference between the two girl twins. Score!

Penny lapped on. And on, and on. She kept her

eyes trained on torsos and sneakers, bouncing her attention from one classmate to the next, careful to avoid eye contact at all costs. She learned that a girl who always had perfectly curled hair and an outfit straight out of a fashion magazine stressed that she presented as a messy slob. A shy girl that Penny had never actually heard speak daydreamed about playing electric guitar onstage in front of thousands of screaming fans. Ryder, the bully who liked to smack the top of Penny's head with his comic book to prove how short she was, claimed he only ate fast food, and always got in trouble for sleeping in class, also shared a bedroom with three younger siblings and desperately missed his dad and wondered when he'd be back. Penny moved on quickly, intuiting that anything more on that topic was Ryder's business, not hers.

Penny had meant to get at least two passes by Gianna, Nayeli, and Rose's table, but she'd been too nervous. Just the thought of them noticing and calling her out for snooping or acting strange or funny or bizarre or anything but completely normal was so mortifying Penny nearly sneezed just thinking about it.

Though not everything Penny heard was

enlightening, much of it was funny. A clique at a center table eagerly discussed their plans to go roller-skating that coming weekend. The girls' thoughts revealed their concerns with logistics like transportation, costumes (roller-skating was a costumed thing, Penny also learned), and arrival time, while the boys' wondered, *Why are Tootsie Pops called Tootsie Pops? What's a Tootsie?*; *I wish someone could just go pee for me*; and *Do whales live in Wales?* The world would be a much sillier place if people actually expressed what was going on in their heads.

"What's your deal, Loose Change?" Max asked the third time she passed by his table. The cafeteria wasn't huge; one very slow lap hardly took any time at all. Lunch was half over and Penny had already completed three loops.

"Slow walking aids digestion," Penny explained quickly, ignoring his one-part-clever, two-parts-rude nickname. Penny could think on her feet like a pro.

"Okay, weirdo," Max retorted, before turning back to Theo and T.C. Tingle, spark, tingle. Penny gripped her Secrets Necklace in her left hand and braced herself to hear Max's potentially not-so-nice thought about her. *T.C. and Theo like each other better than they like me. They're probably hanging out without me all the time, talking about camp and all the fun stuff they did while I was actually being a responsible counselor. They're going to forget about me,* Penny heard Max think. That surprised Penny. Max always seemed like the ringleader of that little threesome. She never would have guessed in a million years that he felt left out by the two boys who followed him around night and day. But that wasn't all. Max didn't have a nasty thing to say about her. He was much more focused on himself and his own problem du jour.

Penny considered taking another slow lap, maybe counterclockwise this time just to shake it up, but her brain felt full. Thank goodness she had control over the activation of the Secrets Necklace—hearing everybody else's thoughts for just a few moments at a time was exhausting! Penny released the charm from her grasp and retreated to the familiar spot at the very corner of the corner table in the cafeteria.

Some of the thoughts Penny heard were hilarious, some were downright informative, but most were surprising. Like being presented with a devil's food cake, only to cut in to find the dense chocolate icing concealed fluffy white cake instead of a rich chocolate center. No, Penny realized, the outside does not always match the inside when it came to seventh grade. With access to a secret world that had always existed beyond her scope, it felt to Penny like being able to breathe underwater.

For a second, Penny felt guilty. Like she was cheating, or stealing secrets, rather. Penny tucked that thought away. It was too much to think of now. She was still a Secrets Necklace amateur, after all.

Just then, the girl with the oversized lime green headphones sat down at the other end of Penny's table. She was in Penny's ELA class, but Penny didn't know her name. In fact, she'd never even heard her speak, though she curiously appeared simultaneously meek and wise. The girl's eyes were very big and very dark brown. She ate a red apple in tiny bites, chewing completely between each baby chomp. She wore a jean jacket, and from the breast pocket she pulled a notebook and a very professional-looking pen. When she took off the cap, Penny saw the tip was no bigger than a grain of table salt. When the girl opened her notebook, Penny saw a drawing depicting a cityscape in such detail it nearly took Penny's breath away. Penny found herself leaning closer to get a better look. The lines of the sketch were so fine they reminded Penny of strands of hair. Penny wondered what urban landscape warranted such care and attention.

Oh, wait a second. Penny didn't actually have to wonder.

Penny brought her finger up to her necklace, placing her tip of her pinky on the small stone at the top of the key-shaped charm. The shade of the girl's eyes, Penny realized, weren't that dissimilar from the color of that stone that Penny had such trouble describing.

Penny listened.

Worst day ever, worst day ever, worst day ever . . . Lime Green Headphones thought.

Huh. Penny listened again to see if she could learn more.

Time move faster, time move faster, time move faster, worst day ever, worst day ever.

Penny dropped her pinky and the echoey thoughts ceased. Penny stole another glance. Lime Green Headphones continued to nibble on her apple and add a line here and a mark there to her already magnificent piece of artwork. Penny sensed the other kids in the cafeteria start to get up, downshifting from lunchtime horseplay vibes back to academic mode. Penny felt a familiar spark in her nose. Then a tingle. Spark, spark, tingle. How could someone with the ability to create such a thorough world with just a pen and piece of paper be having such a terrible day?

Tingle, tingle, spark.

Before Penny could stop herself, she waved her hand to get the girl's attention.

Lime Green Headphones looked up at Penny. Penny waved again. Tingle, spark, spark. The girl slowly exposed part of one ear, keeping the headset mostly on. Penny lightly touched her Secrets Necklace, just in case.

"What city is that?" Penny asked, gesturing to the drawing on the earpiece.

"New York," the girl answered, as if she didn't want to part with the information. Then Penny heard the girl think, *It's me*.

"Wow." Penny felt another spark in her nose. "It's really . . ." Penny searched for the right word. *Beautiful?* Sure. *Detailed?* Obviously. *Astonishing?* Without a doubt. None of those words quite captured the feeling the image inspired. "Real," Penny said. Penny had never been to New York, but the illustration made the pulse of the far-off city feel . . . true. "Alive," Penny added.

"Thanks," the girl peeped. *That's where I'm from,* she thought, but didn't say out loud.

Lime Green Headphones girl still seemed so sad and the sketch of New York City felt more alive each second that passed, so Penny added, "That's your home."

Oops. Penny had just given herself away. The girl hadn't actually *said* she was from New York, she'd just thought it.

"It's my home. I miss it. How did you know?"

"Lucky guess?" Penny's shaky excuse seemed to do the trick. Lime Green Headphones went back to her work. The girl took another bite of her apple, revealing a fleck of the brown seed from deep inside the core. Then Lime Green Headphones smiled. Not at Penny, just to her apple.

Penny gave the key-shaped charm around her neck a little pat, the way she did to Millions sometimes when she walked past the tank on her way to the kitchen, and stood to go.

Penny felt a shy tug on the back of her T-shirt as she walked away.

"I'm Lark," Lime Green Headphones said. Her smile was small, but it was still there.

"Penny." Penny felt the last remnants of a spark in her nose dissolve. She wasn't going to sneeze after all. "That's me."

Penny thought to Secret Necklace Lark one last time, but she had already scuttled away, no longer within eavesdropping range.

Chapter Eight

Penny's fifth-period math class had a substitute that day. They had the choice of watching the same movie about volcanoes (for some reason that was the clip they always showed when her math teacher was out sick or on a "personal day," whatever that meant) or going to the library for a study hall. Obvious choice. Mrs. Notarino, the librarian, was very strict with the whole no-talking policy, but thanks to Otis, Penny knew the school's Wi-Fi password.

Those slow laps during lunch proved mentally draining. Penny hadn't experienced brain overload like that since she'd discovered her first cookbook (Julia Child was a legend but, boy oh boy, did she make roasting a chicken complicated!). She was ready for forty-five minutes of pure, zoned-out, Wi-Fi-connected bliss. Penny settled into an open table toward the back of the room by the outdated encyclopedias, propped up her math book as a shield, and waited for the last episode of her favorite cooking slash travel show to download onto her phone.

The video was 80 percent there when Gianna walked in. To Penny's surprise, she was alone; Nayeli and Rose were nowhere in sight. Gianna sat down a few tables away, pulled out a book, and started to read.

No doubt about it, Gianna was within eavesdropping distance. Penny held her charm and listened.

Peace and quiet, peace and quiet. I need a break from . . . people. Is that bad? Or mean? I hope Rose and Nayeli aren't annoyed with me. Oh gosh, is everyone annoyed with me? Am I the annoying new girl who everyone thinks is annoying? People are probably being nice to me because they feel like they have to. I'm never going to get this geometry homework done. It's too much. Mr. Frost is a maniac, I can't possibly do this by tomorrow. I hope nobody thinks I'm a maniac.

Whoa. Gianna's mind ran a mile a minute. No wonder she needed some peace and quiet in the library. Her inner monologue was relentless. Penny listened on.

I hate being so nervous. I'm the most nervous girl in Lullwater. No, in the whole world. Rose and Nayeli wouldn't even be friends with me if they knew how nervous I am. They are my friends, though, right? All I want to do is go home and watch TV for a million hours. Alone. Why does everything about seventh grade have to be so freaky?!

As if on cue, Nayeli and Rose walked into the library. Penny dropped her charm. Triple tasking—listening with her real ears, listening with her Secrets Necklace, and listening with her eyes (aka watching)—proved oddly challenging.

"There you are," Nayeli exclaimed, way above a whisper.

"Hi, just snuck away to get this awful math homework done," Gianna explained, as cool and collected as always, no trace of her secret preoccupations in her presentation.

"Totally," Rose agreed. "We'll hang."

"Yup, yup," Nayeli confirmed.

Nayeli and Rose sat down. Gianna beamed, as if that's what she wanted all along. Maybe she would make it to the Broadway stage after all. Sooner rather than later.

"So, after school, we were thinking of getting burgers. Wanna?"

"Definitely!" Gianna agreed.

"No talking in the library!" Mrs. Notarino hissed from her desk. She'd mastered the art of the scream whisper.

Nayeli, Rose, and Gianna giggled and scooched their chairs closer together. The girls whispered at a decidedly undetectable volume. Gianna's peace and quiet had come to an end.

Penny's phone vibrated, indicating her download was complete. She tucked in her earbuds and pressed Play, careful to hide from Mrs. Notarino's watchful eye.

But Penny couldn't focus on her show. Gianna's inner monologue tumbled through her brain. Penny simply couldn't believe what she'd heard. Or eavesdropped. Was "Secret Necklaced" the right verb? It didn't matter. Gianna King: nervous? Afraid she didn't have friends? Out of sorts with the whole concept of seventh grade? That just did not compute. Gianna was the friendliest, most confident seventh grader at Lullwater Middle School. How could any of that possibly be true?

When Penny left the library, Gianna, Nayeli, and Rose still sat gossiping and giggling and doing whatever trios of friends do. Spark, spark, spark. Tingle, tingle, tingle. Penny didn't even try to stifle her sneeze.

"Sshhhh," Mrs. Notarino screeched. "No sounds in the library!"

"Bless you," Gianna whispered. Penny glanced over, and Gianna met her gaze with the most genuine, confident, and carefree smile that Penny had ever seen.

"Thanks," Penny whispered, too quiet for Gianna, the librarian, or anyone without a Secrets Necklace of their own to hear.

Chapter Nine

Otis texted on Penny's way home. Where ya been Ghost Pepp?

Where have YOU been? Penny thought. Before Penny could come up with a less bratty way to communicate that she missed Otis (without actually saying that she missed him; that seemed a bit babyish), another text came in.

Make so many new friends you forget about me? Lol. Keep it weird.

Otis's text felt like a finger prick. For a reason she couldn't identify, Penny wanted to throw her phone across the street. Bonus points if Otis was across the street and the phone smacked him on his chopping hand.

When Penny got home, she immediately went to the magnolia tree. That was the only chance she had of calming down; she was too riled up to even bake (Penny had once tried to cook angry, and let's just say it ended in . . . fire). She climbed up to the branch shaped like a bat wing, but couldn't get comfortable. So she climbed higher. And higher, and then a little higher. She inched her way to the back end of the tree, the side farthest from her house. For some reason she never climbed up or down that portion of the trunk. Penny dripped sweat by the time she stopped, despite the slight chill in the air. Maybe fall was coming after all. The key-shaped charm around her neck clung to her clammy skin. Penny settled on a new branch, high up, one that reminded her of a slingshot. She held the charm in her hand, though there wasn't a soul within remote eavesdropping distance. Despite being near the peak of the tree, the leaves were still thick. Penny was concealed. Finally, as she ran her finger over the key-shaped charm's cool surface, her anger began to dissipate.

Max feels left out.

Cole truly believes flexing his biceps will result in more armpit hair.

Lark might be the best artist since Frida Kahlo.

Gianna King and I have something in common,

Penny realized. *Gianna King is just as nervous as me.* The revelation nearly took her breath away.

"Gianna King is just as nervous as Penny Hoppe," Penny said to her hollow magnolia universe, to see if their shared secret felt real. It did. "Gianna King is just as nervous as Penny Hoppe," she repeated. Her voice started as a whisper, but gained strength as she went. Penny closed her eyes and repeated the phrase a third time, this time yelling, "Gianna King is just as nervous as Penny Hoppe!" Penny imagined her words were purple food coloring seeping into crevices between branches and waxy leaves with each syllable she spoke, saturating every space inside her magnolia tree universe.

For the first time since August 30, Penny didn't feel so alone. This Secrets Necklace was great. Better than great. Truly magnificent.

Penny smiled. And then she laughed. Once she started she couldn't stop. Penny remembered her prior friend-making attempts. More like friend-making fails. But now she had a secret weapon. A secret ingredient. A Secrets Necklace. And Penny Hoppe knew better than anyone that sometimes a secret ingredient could make all the difference.

That evening, Penny took another stab at Project Better than the Box. Inspired by her first day Secret Necklacing, Penny chose to be methodical. She pulled out two cookbooks from the shelves above the microwave, a newer one and another that functioned more as a culinary encyclopedia. The differences between the recipes for yellow cake in each cookbook were minor, but, as Penny had come to learn, even a tiny change could prove significant. When it came to baking, that is. Two eggs here, three eggs there. Room-temperature butter in one, melted butter in the other. Though Penny's previous attempts were close, it finally occurred to her that combining various, proven recipes rather than baking willy-nilly on instinct might be the way to go. So far, both in and out of the kitchen, Penny's instincts hadn't exactly served her well.

Penny mixed up the batter and poured it into a rectangular cake pan, placed the concoction on the middle oven rack, and waited patiently at the kitchen table. Sylvia sat next to her, absorbed in her crossword puzzle.

"Is it okay to cheat at other things besides horse

racing?" Penny asked. The sweet smell of baking cake filled the room. It was almost ready.

"Don't ask questions you know the answer to," Sylvia said.

"Six across is *ladle*," Penny stated. Obviously. *Soup spoon*. What else could it be? "And I don't know the answer. That's why I'm asking."

Sylvia sighed and put down her pencil. "Cheating is a personal thing. You have to come up with your own set of rules." Sylvia then gave Penny a look that indicated she was done talking, and went back to her puzzle. "I would have gotten *ladle* without your help, you know," she muttered.

When Penny took her PBttB attempt out of the oven, she knew it wasn't right. The outside was perfectly golden, but it deflated a bit in the middle. She cut a piece for her and Sylvia to share anyway.

"Needs icing," Sylvia demanded after taking a bite.

"Yes, it's dry," Penny agreed.

Because Sylvia wasn't wrong, and because Penny wasn't going to let a cake go to waste, subpar as it was, she whipped up a batch of chocolate buttercream frosting. Mind preoccupied on what error she might have made (maybe three cups was just a hair too much flour after all), Penny absentmindedly tossed some micro-wave-softened butter, several handfuls of powdered sugar, a glug of milk, a few scoops of cocoa, and a quick spill of vanilla extract into a bowl and whisked away.

The frosting turned out fantastic, but Penny hardly noticed. Project Better than the Box was starting to officially feel more like Mystery-of-the-Box. And Penny was not a huge fan of mysteries.

Before bed, Penny remembered Otis's texts from that afternoon. She'd never responded. The finger prick from his earlier text now only pinched when she thought about it. Penny could handle a little pinch.

Penny didn't have so many friends. Not yet. But she had a secret weapon. Her Secrets Necklace could single-handedly turn her friend-making attempts to friend-making successes.

Despite the late hour, Penny felt a surge of adrenaline. With this magic necklace, seventh grade was going to turn around for her. She just knew it. Penny typed a text into her phone.

PBttB almost near completion. You better bring it. She hit Send with no regrets.

Chapter ten

Penny didn't exactly have a friend-making-Secrets-Necklace-combo-platter plan. Not yet. Fortunately, a perfect friend-making-Secrets-Necklace-combo-platter opportunity presented itself later that week after school.

Penny sat on the hill behind the East Hallway that overlooked the athletic field. It was a beautiful day: seventy-two degrees, sunny, not a cloud in the sky, not a mosquito in sight. School had let out nearly twenty minutes ago, but Penny wasn't quite ready to go home yet. Sylvia and the lizards would be waiting (well, not waiting . . . physically present was the more accurate description) whenever she got there. She'd do a veggie stir-fry for dinner, which required a minimal amount of prep. So Penny luxuriated in the mid-afternoon sun and retrieved her poetry journal from her backpack.

Penny hadn't forgotten about the poetry reading coming up. The event loomed on the horizon like a dull toothache. Though participation wasn't mandatory, Penny needed to compose an alternate, less personal draft of her "Where I'm From" poem, just in case she sneezed her way into the spotlight again. Two lines into the alternate poem and Penny was stuck, stuck, stuck. The words didn't flow the way they had when she'd written the original draft—the sincere and private one that belonged to her and her alone.

Penny had tentatively titled the new piece "Plum Street." Even revealing the name of the street where she lived felt a bit too exposing. Not because she thought anyone in Lullwater had stalker tendencies, but because even just printing those two words evoked emotion in Penny. "Plum Street" was a tree-lined road where she knew every bump in the asphalt and could recognize her driveway blindfolded because of the way the moss lining the driveway smelled. It was the street where she'd forced Otis to supervise her first lemonade sale (at ten cents a cup, she sold her product way below market value), and the place where she'd knocked out her front two (baby) teeth after a spill graduating from two training wheels to two big wheels. In short, Plum Street had history. Plum Street was familiar. Like Lark's drawing of New York, Plum Street for Penny was capital "H" Home. All in all, "Plum Street," both the two-word combination and the feelings it brought up was a piece of her heart she didn't want to escape.

Penny erased the title. The tip of her dull pencil hovered over the newly blank space. Instead of words, she drew a rectangular box around where the erased title had been. She'd fill it in later.

Penny took a deep breath, and lay on her back. The grass itched the backs of her arms, but the overhead sun was worth it, so she stayed put. Penny flipped back a page in her poetry journal. She was about to read the original poem to herself again, just for inspiration, when a soccer ball dropped from the sky and onto her stomach.

It didn't hurt as much as Penny would have thought, but it didn't feel great, either.

"You're chasing!" Penny heard a voice call from behind her. Penny turned around and saw Shaylah, Reem, and the other soccer girl with red hair coming down the hill behind her.

"Sorry," Shaylah called. "Hollis thinks it's cool to kick balls to outer space if she feels like it, but I'm not running after them!" So the red-haired girl was Hollis. Good to know.

"All good," Penny said. The sting on her stomach was starting to fade.

"Dude, I was practicing my punt," Hollis argued.

"Keepers," Reem said, rolling her eyes. Whatever that meant.

Penny watched as they neared, presumably to retrieve the ball Penny held in her hands. It was then that Penny remembered her necklace. Eavesdropping distance . . . check. Fingertips touching the chilly charm . . . affirmative. Penny smiled at the soccer girls, and while they continued to approach, she listened.

That's the girl who was so amped about the World Cup, Hollis thought. Penny perked up. Hollis remembered her! Maybe her previous friend-making attempt hadn't been so bad after all!

Shooting practice is going to be a nightmare. Reem has no aim, Penny heard Shaylah think. Hmmm. Shooting practice. Penny glanced at the field at the bottom of the hill. The white goal posts at the ends of the pitch (pitch—fancy soccer term for field!) glistened.

No way am I running after all the shots Shaylah shanks, Reem thought. *That's on her.*

A moment later, the girls stood by Penny, who remained seated on the grass. "Here you go," Penny said, tossing the ball to Hollis and keeping one hand on her charm. Reem and Shaylah each had a soccer ball at their feet. Instead of catching the ball in her hands, Hollis received the toss on her thigh and brought it to the ground with her right foot. *Fancy*, Penny thought.

"Thanks. Sorry about before," Hollis said.

The teammates continued on toward the field. Penny took one last listen.

Feet hurt, legs hurt, so tired. I swear if Shaylah doesn't get her shots on frame . . . I'm over this already, Reem thought.

Give me an H! You got your H, you got your H. Hollis, similar to Cole, secretly gave herself pump-up speeches. Hollis's version proved way more endearing than Cole's ridiculous chant.

We could really use a ball chaser. All varsity teams have them. A robot or a ball chaser, Penny heard

Shaylah think a moment later, right before the trio faded out of eavesdropping distance.

That gave Penny an idea. *I could be that robot*, she thought.

"Hey!" Penny shouted. Then, a little louder, because her initial greeting failed to get their attention. "Soccer stars!" That worked. Shaylah, Reem, and Hollis stopped and turned around. "Can I join?"

"Umm . . . I mean we're really trying to get a lot of touches in. Do you even play soccer?" Hollis asked.

"I . . . I feel like running around. It's too nice of a day to stay still," Penny vamped. "What if I"—she paused for effect—"ball chase for y'all?"

"Really?" Shaylah asked.

"Totes!" Penny said. She tossed her poetry journal into her open backpack and trotted down the hill. Once in closer proximity, Penny took the opportunity to quickly listen in.

She def does not play soccer, Hollis thought.

Who would want to be a ball chaser? Reem thought. Penny almost raised her hand and said "Me!" before remembering she'd heard Reem *think*, not *speak*.

"I really don't mind," Penny said.

"Okay. Cool," Hollis said, warming up to the idea.

Shaylah added, "That's . . . so nice of you. Thanks . . ."

"Penny."

"Thanks, Penny," Reem said, then thought, *Penny might be an angel.*

"You got your work cut out for you. Shaylah can't hit a target to save her life," Reem whispered a few paces later. Penny smiled, happy to be included in some teammate gossip already.

To be fair, Penny had volunteered to ball chase without knowing exactly what that would entail. Basically, every time Reem or Shaylah took a shot on goal (Hollis was the goalie) and missed, Penny had to fetch the ball and bring it back. The girls set up a dozen or so cones all around the box (or the eighteen—another soccer fact Penny remembered from her research) to serve as imaginary defenders. Sometimes they narrowly missed the goal, and sometimes, especially in Shaylah's case, the ball sailed over the crossbar and into . . . not *not* outer space.

Penny definitely got her sweat on; she was winded within minutes. Luckily, Reem, Shaylah, and Hollis were all still wiped from sprints they'd done a few days ago, so they took lots of breaks.

As it turned out, soccer girls didn't just talk about soccer. They discussed homework (Penny could relate), their annoying siblings (Penny did not think she could relate), the boys they had crushes on (some guys with silly nicknames that went to a different school but who also played soccer—Penny desperately wanted to relate), and ponytail length (Penny's shaggy bangs had inspired the topic of conversation). Every now and then Penny piped in with an "uh-huh" or a "you bet." She wasn't able to Secret Necklace at all because most of the time she was chasing after or holding one to three soccer balls at once.

"I'm pooped. Let's call it a day," Reem suggested after a half hour.

Penny was too out of breath to speak, but she nodded vigorously. She hoped they saw her.

"Fine by me," Shaylah agreed.

Hollis gave a thumbs-up. The girls headed over to the sideline where they'd dropped their school and soccer gear.

"That's a pretty necklace," Shaylah said while en route. Penny instinctively brought her hand to the charm. It felt about twenty degrees cooler than the air. "What is it the key to?"

"Your hearrrrrttt?" Hollis joked.

Tingle, tingle, spark.

"Just something I stumbled upon. Vintage," Penny answered. That seemed to impress them.

"So what's, like, your thing?" Hollis asked while they packed up to go. The soccer girls sat in the grass among their strewn about backpacks, removing their sweaty socks and cleats. Penny stood awkwardly, wishing she had cleats or some other form of footwear to remove.

"What do you mean?" Penny asked. Spark, spark. Suddenly on the spot, Penny wished there were more soccer balls to chase.

"I dunno. Like, what do you do?"

Penny hesitated. Her thing was cooking, right? That's what she loved to do. But she wasn't on a team or anything. So did it count? It wasn't like she competed in it, and it's not like she got paid to do it, like Otis.

Tingle, spark, tingle.

"A little bit of this, a little bit of that," Penny

evaded. She made a point to chuckle, in case there was a way for her answer to present as funny and not odd. She was failing again. She needed her necklace to come to the rescue.

Spark, spark, spark.

Penny moved her right hand toward her neck to make contact with the charm, but Reem, ever the athlete, intercepted her.

"Ball chaser extraordinaire!" Reem exclaimed, grabbing Penny's right wrist and raising it over her head, as if she were a champion boxer.

Penny sneezed anyway.

"Bless ya," Shaylah said, and gestured to the expanse of field around them. "Tons of allergies out here in Grasslandia."

If only that were it, Penny thought, grateful nobody could hear *her* thoughts, only to discover the real source of her outburst.

A few minutes later, cleats were off, balls were gathered, and the girls were ready to go.

"I got the cones," Penny offered, hoping to extend her first official soccer girl hang a few minutes longer.

"Rad. We just gotta drop them in the gym with the

balls. Our coach is so stingy about materials. It's like, hello, do you want us to practice on our own time or not?"

Penny laughed and reached down to pick up the stack of orange cones that actually looked more like disks.

"Your backpack's open," Hollis noted.

"Thanks!" Penny chirped. She paused to zip it up, but the girls were already several steps ahead, so she left it open. She'd deal with it later. Penny didn't want to be left behind. All she had in her bag was her poetry journal and some textbooks, and, frankly, Penny would be thrilled to never see anything geometry related ever again. Penny grabbed the cones and trotted to catch up.

On her way up the hill, Penny saw Lark, the artist from slow-lap day in the cafeteria, coming in the opposite direction. She didn't take the girl with the giant lime green headphones to be the sporty type, but then again, before ball chasing, neither was Penny. Lark gave Penny a shy wave as she passed by. Penny's hands were full of cones, so all she could do was nod and offer a quick smile in return.

Penny was exhausted by the time she got home. It took all her energy to chop up some broccoli, carrots, and onion. Her hang with the soccer girls had gone well. She had no regrets, no moments that she wished she could take back or that caused her to grimace upon reflection. She'd taken some real strides forward in the friend-making department. She was pretty sure she'd be invited back to ball chase next time the girls had shooting practice. As Hollis might say, was ball chasing her thing? Penny didn't think so, but at the end of the day, did it really matter? She'd spent her afternoon with the company of others. She didn't know if they were her friends yet, but they had one hang down. That was certainly better than nothing.

She waited on the rice to finish steaming, and combined ingredients for a stir-fry sauce (soy sauce, honey, rice wine vinegar, and a dash of chili oil). A photo of a pathetic, frosting-less cake popped up on her phone.

Hashtag PBttB epic fail, the caption read.

Penny smiled. She felt guilty laughing, but that was one horrible-looking cake. The edges were burned and the center was cracked, creating a canyon of sorts. Oof.

Don't show chef. Fired on the spot, Penny replied.

Ellipses appeared right away, indicating Otis was typing, but then vanished. No response came through. Penny waited, but he wrote nothing back. Maybe a ten top (table of ten) had just put in their order. Or maybe Otis was joking with his new kitchen friends, replacing the whipped cream with mayo or something like that. In case it was the other possibility, that Otis took her jest to heart, Penny followed up: jk, jk. Not over yet. Then, PS try more b-soda, fool <B.

Otis hated emojis. Manual hearts over cartoon hearts for life, they agreed. It felt good to remember something else she shared with her big brother.

Chapter Eleven

A few days later Ms. Samich returned for poetry class, a week after Penny's disastrous sneeze. Penny spent the first part of class Secret Necklacing her little heart out. She found her nose was less likely to tingle when her attention was on others. Aka when she was listening to her classmates' thoughts. Ms. Samich began class with a video clip of some old poet reading their work on a stage, so no actual participation was required. It was really the perfect opportunity to drift away to Secrets Necklace mode. So far, Penny'd acquired the following insights:

Jane had a habit of counting the number of letters in words she saw around the room when she zoned out.

Theo really wanted to cheat on his history quiz because he hadn't studied, but was afraid of the karmic impact that might have on his life.

Mateo left his lucky shorts at his mom's house, which he wouldn't be able to get for another week until his stay at his dad's house was over, so maybe he should find a new pair of lucky shorts because that was simply too long to go without.

T.C. had a scissors phobia and missed his childhood horse, Jasmine Belle.

Rose's and Nayeli's minds both wandered to possible outfit choices for a social gathering that coming weekend.

Gianna wondered if her friends from her old school in Atlanta still remembered her. Penny scoffed at that insight at first. The idea of forgetting Gianna King seemed implausible to Penny.

"Okay, time to put pencil to the paper," Ms. Samich announced, turning the SMART Board off and the lights back on. "I would like y'all to do a free write—who remembers what a free write is?"

"Write whatever comes to mind, even if it doesn't make sense, without stopping," Mateo said without raising his hand. What a suck-up. "Don't worry about grammar or spelling and definitely don't sensor yourself."

"Bingo." Ms. Samich was starting to find her

groove, Penny noted. What she wouldn't give to be able to hear the inner workings of her poetry teacher's mind . . . alas . . . "You don't need your poetry journals today."

"Good, because I lost mine!" Cole said under his breath from the back. His clowning was rewarded with a few snickers and a lone giggle. Ms. Samich didn't seem to hear. Or care.

"I'm passing out pieces of paper—line free, of course. I don't want you all to feel too precious about this, which is why we're not working in our journals today. This is just an exercise, so feel free to tell it all to the page. Express yourself without worrying about how it sounds." Penny heard another snicker. Quickly she grabbed her charm and pretended to stretch so she could turn around and properly place her attention on Cole.

Turkey Club will hate me when she finds out I can't spell. Penny heard Cole think. Then, *Why don't letters make more sense? They're so jumbly.*

Ms. Samich dropped a blank page on Cole's desk. He immediately folded it into a paper airplane and launched it across the room.

"If you need another piece of paper, just raise your

hand and I'll bring one by. And without further ado, on your mark . . . get set . . . free write!"

Penny brought her pencil to the paper and paused. The paper was so . . . empty. Vast. It felt too big to fill. Tingle. Not one to break rules, Penny followed the free write instructions: She kept her pencil moving, relaying to the page whatever came to mind.

Ten minutes later, Ms. Samich said, "And pencils down."

Penny's page was nearly filled. Not with words, but with small loops and squiggles, neatly scrawled across the page. Penny had technically followed the instructions. She wrote what came to mind. Problem was, her mind was a jumble of other people's thoughts and sparks and tingles. None of that came out in the form of actual words.

"We have time for one quick reading," Ms. Samich said innocently. Penny looked down at her paper. She blinked through an onset of tingles. She obviously had nothing to read. Spark, spark. "Penny H., do you want to give it another shot today?"

"Umm . . ." No, Penny did not want to give it another shot. Tingles and sparks pinballed around in her nose.

"Excuse me, Ms. Samich, but class is technically over," Lark squeaked from the other side of the room. Her voice was barely audible, absorbed by the classroom's stale air.

Ms. Samich looked at the clock, then at her watch, then back at the clock, as if her disorientation could turn back time.

"Good catch. Boy, time flies when you're free writing!" Penny took it back. Ms. Samich was not getting the hang of things. "Next time, Penny H. That's a bet." Ms. Samich looked Penny in the eye and nodded. Penny could only hold her gaze for a second before an onset of sparks forced her to look away.

That moment, Penny thought to Secret Necklace Gianna. *Phew*, she heard Gianna think, before she skipped out of the room, arms looped with Nayeli and Rose. Penny bounded out the door, not thinking to thank Lark for the life preserver.

Chapter twelve

Over the next week, Penny seized every opportunity to use the Secrets Necklace to her friend-making advantage. She'd had trouble getting within organic eavesdropping distance of Gianna again, which was frustrating, but a run-in with Lark in the bathroom revealed Lark's craving for chocolate, which was something they had in common at that moment, so that felt nice. Her ball-chasing escapade with the soccer girls had gone so well (Hollis and Shaylah both said "hi" to her when they passed in the hallway the next day!) that Penny figured she'd try again with the Gang of Compounding Scientists. Best to diversify her emerging friend group. The soccer girls would likely have busy schedules with practices and games and all, so having some non-athletes on her roster seemed wise.

She encountered the gang in the Cavern after

school. Penny leaned against the brick wall next to the school's entrance, fanning herself with her science test (A-!). The temperature was finally starting to mellow, but Penny Hoppe still ran hot. She fiddled with her charm, gliding it back and forth on the chain. The Gang of Compounding Scientists—Jane, Janiyah, Sullivan, and Samson—emerged out the double doors.

"I just don't think we can call ourselves the Gang of Compounding Scientists unless we actually do scientific things," Samson said. His twin and the girls followed him to the far corner of the Cavern and sat in a diamond configuration, Janiyah across from Samson, Jane across from Sullivan. The Cavern was unusually empty that afternoon; most sports practices and actual school-sponsored clubs had started that week, so many of the students at Lullwater Middle School were otherwise occupied or had already caught the bus home. The vacancy of the space made for great eavesdropping—both Secrets Necklace style and the old-fashioned way. "Which is why I think our next order of business should be to put the gummy vitamin challenge to the test in the form of an actual experiment with controls and variables and the whole shebang."

Penny desperately wanted to know the backstory of this gummy vitamin challenge, but none of their thoughts yielded such information.

Instead, Penny heard Jane think, *Samson's got to drop this whole Gang of whatever Scientists thing. It's so not happening. I don't get why J is so into it.*

The bottle says no more than two a day, but will twelve actually kill me? Sullivan wondered. Then, in a British accent for some reason, Sullivan said, "I think we're known far and wide as scientists." And then, *Ooh, room filled of low-concentration gummy vitamins so you can't overdo it—Fantasy Dream House hall of fame right there!*

"Agreed, our reputation is solid," Janiyah added, and then thought, *Samson's eyes just sparkle in this light.* Penny looked at Samson to confirm. The dim Cavern shade did nothing for his appearance as far as Penny was concerned.

Samson persevered. "Look, it's either revisiting the periodic table—which I know y'all are slacking on—" The other three members of the club averted their eyes.

No science allowed in my fantasy dream house, Penny heard Jane think. Wow, they really loved that

Fantasy Dream House game and were really not that into science, for the most part.

Samson continued, "Or we devise a proper experiment to determine the risks and rewards of an accurately executed gummy vitamin challenge."

The other three's thoughts were a combination of *Noooooo, Whyyyyy?*, and *Anything for you!* (Janiyah, obviously).

"Let's take a vote, 'cause democracy, duh. All in favor of the gummy vitamin—"

Before Samson could finish his voting instructions, Penny placed her attention on Jane just in time to hear her think, *Someone save us.*

Okay, Penny thought. *I got you. Penny Hoppe to the rescue!*

"Hey, y'all!" Penny said, sauntering over. Mini spark, medium tingle. "I don't know what kind of official Gang of Compounding Scientist stuff y'all have planned," she said, playing dumb (spark, spark, megaspark). Before she chickened out or the sparks increased (whichever came first), Penny offered, "But anybody up for a rousing game of Fantasy Dream House?"

"Yes, please!" Sullivan and Jane said in unison.

"Well, okay," Janiyah added a moment later.

"Democracy," Jane explained, elbowing Samson's side.

Samson rolled his eyes. "Fine," he said, and then thought, *All fun and games now, but they'll be jealous when I get my full ride to MIT.*

Penny saw a space in the diamond configuration between Samson and Jane, the one spot not shaded by the Cavern's overhang. Penny was about to take the seat in the sun when she had another idea.

"Hey, do you mind switching?" Penny asked Janiyah, motioning to the sun-drenched space of concrete next to Samson with her non-Secrets-Necklace-engaged hand. By way of explanation, she offered, "I run hot."

"Oh, okay," Janiyah said nervously, though she quickly jumped up to exchange places. *Make sure your knees don't touch, make sure your knees don't touch. Then he'll know you love him,* Penny heard Janiyah think as she claimed her new seat in the configuration. "Happy to help!"

Penny plopped down across from Samson and watched Janiyah carefully ease herself into her new sunny place in the diamond turned pentagon. Her knee came within millimeters of Samson's, but no contact was made. *Close call*, Janiyah thought once she'd finally settled. Penny saw her cheeks were flushed, likely not from the sun.

"If we're doing this, let's make it a speed round," Samson suggested. More like ordered. He liked being the boss, Penny gathered.

"Oooh, fun. We haven't done one of those in a while," Janiyah said.

"Bring it," Jane replied, sitting up a little straighter in preparation.

"What's a speed round?" Penny had the feeling the leisurely game was about to turn athletic.

"Competitive version," Samson answered. "Go around the circle, name an addition to your fantasy dream house, boom, boom, boom, go, go, go. If you pause and break the rhythm, you're out."

"Okay." Sounded like a weird game to be competitive about, but Penny didn't protest. Now that she was officially a ball-chaser extraordinaire, she felt more confident in her overall competitive sport abilities— both of the mind and the body. The soccer girls and the Gang of Compounding Scientists had a lot more in common than probably either group realized.

"You'll get the hang of it," Janiyah assured.

The speed round started off slow. The pace of a minuet, if Penny remembered her musical terms correctly. Each full revolution around the pentagon, though, the beat picked up. Penny kept her left hand on her charm, but it proved impossible to listen in on thoughts, pay attention to the game, and throw out a new fantasy dream house offering every round.

Many of the crew's fantasy dream house ideas were not what Penny would put in a house entirely of her own fantastical design. But when her first contribution of "a room with a bigger lizard tank for my pets," was met with unimpressed facial expressions from all (Penny didn't have time to Secret Necklace what they were *really* thinking), she decided to take her cues from the experts. Play it safe.

Three revolutions around the pentagon, and they were on fire. Penny struggled to keep up.

"Bed made with the bubbles from bubble tea," Samson said.

"TV that doesn't hurt your eyes if you look at it for too long," Janiyah said.

"Aquarium full of baby seahorses," Jane said.

Penny's turn. "Unicorns!" Penny said, sticking with the animal theme.

Sullivan picked up, without missing a beat. "A room filled with instruments that has a potion you can drink that makes you a master at all the instruments."

"Windows made of ice," Samson declared. *That was a weird one*, Penny thought, but who was she to judge?

"Another potion you can drink that allows you to smell what you hear," Janiyah declared. Penny let out a chuckle. That sounded more like a deranged riddle than anything else. This fantasy dream house was getting weirder. And Penny Hoppe liked weird.

"Aaaaa—" Jane dragged out the vowel, presumably to buy time. "Hair dryer that dries your hair in four seconds flat and makes it either curly or straight. That's also glow-in-the-dark." Janiyah gave her sister a high five. The twins had very thick hair. Such a tool would certainly come in handy.

Samson clapped his hands across the circle. Shoot. Penny's turn. How could she build off a magic hair dryer? And did that even count? They were playing Fantasy Dream House, not Fantasy Dream Beauty Tool.

"Uhmmm, scissors that never give you a bad haircut," Penny stammered. She'd gotten her answer in just in the nick of time.

Penny hesitated again the next time her turn came up. *A kitchen with a drawer full of Japanese knives*, is what she wanted to say, but since she assumed none of her Fantasy Dream House companions knew much about the value of a carbon-steel chef's knife, she feared she'd come across as a murderer.

"Aaaand, that's time," Samson interjected.

She'd paused for too long. Penny was out. She scooted back a foot, completely out of the pentagon. The sun had shifted. A sharp ray of sun scorched Penny's back through her T-shirt.

Penny watched as the gang of four played a couple more speed rounds. She held her charm and tried to listen in, but at that point the game was moving so quickly, the only thoughts between turns proved to be exactly what came out of the participants' mouths.

Janiyah was out next. She leaned behind Jane's back and affectionately tapped Penny's shoulder. She confided, "Don't feel bad, we've been playing this for years. Plus, it helps if you're a twin." Penny wasn't sure she understood what twindom had to do with it, but she believed her.

"And if you stockpile fantasy dream house elements in your free time," Jane grumbled after she faltered on her next turn, nodding her head toward the boys. "Like these two clowns."

But Penny didn't feel bad that she'd lost. She felt bad that she'd worked so hard to come up with fantasies that weren't her own. The feeling felt similar to the one she'd had the other day when she tried to compose the backup draft of her poem, before she got sucked into ball chasing. Penny made a mental note to consider some top-notch fantasy dream house ideas to keep in her back pocket, for a speed round or otherwise.

Still, the spot on her shoulder that Janiyah touched tingled for the rest of the day, and not in a sneeze-related way. She'd come, she'd dreamed, and though she hadn't necessarily conquered, the effort was nothing to be ashamed of. Despite the hollow ping that stubbornly remained in the pit of her stomach, Penny tried to remember that her friend-making encounter with the Gang of Compounding Scientists was a success.

Chapter Thirteen

Penny's big chance with Gianna came that Friday in Ms. Samich's class. To make up for a session she'd missed when sick, it was Ms. Samich's second class that week. It had been a particularly rowdy period. Ms. Samich had lost control several times, to the point where Mr. Turney had to step in (when Ms. Samich taught, he had a habit of retreating behind his desk to grade papers and sigh) and scream until his face turned red. Mr. Turney probably needed a new job. He was going to have a heart attack soon, Penny feared. Or at the very least, throw Cole out the window. That would probably make Cole's day, now that Penny thought about it. Since Penny'd learned how jumbled words got inside his brain, she did feel a bit more sympathetic toward him. Still, he was a C-list class clown and not *not* obnoxious.

Ms. Samich dedicated that Friday's class to revision.

"Remember your delicious details, awesome adjectives, and vivid verbs!" Ms. Samich encouraged as she whooshed around the room. Her long dress had already snagged a stapler and the corner of the wastebasket.

"And don't deny alliteration," Mateo added, laughing at his own joke.

"Next session will be our rehearsal before the big reading. So use this time to finalize your work."

It'd taken Penny a good ten minutes of searching in her backpack to concede to the fact that she must have left her poetry journal at home. At first, she'd cursed herself for the mistake, but then realized that the new draft of her "Where I'm From" poem was basically nonexistent, so just starting from scratch on a scrap piece of paper wasn't the worst thing. When Ms. Samich began her campaign for people "who we haven't heard from" to share work, Penny only had a few pathetic lines.

Sparks and tingles for days.

"If you're nervous, practicing now will make

presenting in the auditorium much, much easier, I promise."

"And be sure to project," Mr. Turney piped in from behind his desk. "I've just been informed that the stand microphone went missing after the last assembly. Again."

"No microphone?" Ms. Samich asked. Her eyes widened and her body stiffened. "I was promised we'd have a mic."

Ms. Samich approached Mr. Turney's desk. While the two frantically whispered about logistics, chatter spread across the classroom quicker than spilled soup. Penny remained a bit preoccupied, wondering where exactly she'd left her poetry journal (maybe on the floor by the lizard tank or on the kitchen table underneath one of Sylvia's crosswords?), but Nayeli, Rose, and Gianna's conversation managed to pierce her worry. "You should read yours, Gianna, it's, like, so good," Nayeli insisted.

"Yeah, if mine was half as good, I'd basically be shouting it from the rooftops!" Rose agreed.

Penny watched Gianna's cheeks blush bright red. She smiled, without her teeth, and brushed her friends off. "Oh, it's nothing that special."

Gianna was nervous, Penny could tell. And she didn't need her Secrets Necklace to know that. Still, might as well . . .

Penny tangled her fingers into the silver chain, the key resting against the back of her hand.

Omg no, no, no, no. I can't. No, she heard Gianna think. Her building panic sounded very familiar.

But Nayeli was persistent. "C'mon, you *have* to. That line about your little brother is so funny, Gianna."

"Gianna, did I hear that you'd like to share?" Oh man. Ms. Samich. Gianna was basically entering her worst nightmare, Penny realized.

"Uhmmm," Gianna stalled.

No, no, no. How do I say no? I don't want to disappoint her but no, no, no.

"C'mon, do it!" Nayeli encouraged. "You're such a good actor!"

This isn't acting, this isn't acting, nothing like acting, there's no lights and no stage and no, no, no, no.

"We'd love to hear your work," Ms. Samich added.

Gianna smiled again and shifted in her seat. She looked so uncomfortable and anxious. Penny knew the feeling. She knew the feeling well.

"If you want," Penny interjected, taking a cue from Mateo and not raising her hand, "I'll read it for you."

"Oh, what a lovely idea. We haven't heard from you yet, either, Penny H. Would you prefer that, Gianna?"

"Okay," Gianna said tentatively.

Penny didn't have time to Secret Necklace Gianna again before Ms. Samich ushered her up to the front of the classroom. Penny tried to catch Gianna's eye so she'd know everything was going to be a-okay, but Gianna still had that deer-in-headlights look. *It probably hasn't hit her yet that she's off the hook*, Penny thought. As Penny well knew, sometimes it took a minute for fear-based adrenaline to relent.

Penny picked up Gianna's poem from her desk (Gianna didn't hand it to her—she was probably still all riled up), and faced the class, just as she had on that horrible sneezy day a couple weeks prior. No spark, no tingle. Penny gazed down at Gianna's handwriting—loopy, stylish, and easy to read. Still, no spark, no tingle. Penny looked up at Gianna, who still appeared moderately flabbergasted. Penny wished that Gianna, too, had a Secrets Necklace so she'd know a crisis had been avoided. *I'm going to knock it out of the park for you, G*, Penny thought as she took a deep breath. She began.

As it turned out, reading someone else's poem was not terribly sneeze-inducing for Penny Hoppe. In fact, she had fun. A blast, actually.

Gianna's poem was good. One of the very first lines, a description of her brother—"a tiny fart machine with a heart of gold"—sent a wave of laughter through the audience. Not the kind of laughter that made Penny feel sneezy. A totally different kind. This laughter felt like encouragement.

Penny managed to sneak in a quick Secret Necklace while she waited for the chuckles to die down, just to get some real-time feedback. She was overjoyed when she heard *Whoa, Penny's funny* and *She should take Mr. Turney's place.* Encouraged by information she'd received courtesy of the necklace, Penny hammed it up a couple lines later, putting on her best old lady voice when Gianna described her great-aunt. She didn't have time to Secret Necklace anyone again, but the class was silent as midnight in the mountains, and Penny could tell she had her classmates' rapt attention. Penny continued to perform Gianna's poem, confidence and dramatic commitment only building with each syllable.

"Atlanta, Atlanta, Atlanta, home sweet—" Penny paused for dramatic effect. *"Home."*

Everybody clapped. Penny could see no other option but to take a bow.

"Very nice reading, Penny H.," Ms. Samich said. If Penny wasn't mistaken, Ms. Samich looked impressed.

"Thanks!" Penny said. For the first time since August 30, the beginning of seventh grade, Penny felt like a million bucks. She bounced over to Gianna, beaming, and handed back her poem.

"It's really good," she confirmed.

She waited for Gianna to return the compliment; Penny had a feeling her performance was of equal quality. Instead, Gianna gave her a tight-lipped smile, snatched her poetry journal from Penny's hands, and shoved it into her backpack.

Huh, that wasn't exactly the reaction that Penny expected.

"Can I go next?" Mateo begged.

Ms. Samich looked at the clock. "Well . . . okay. I suppose we have a few minutes left."

Once back in her seat, Penny immediately grasped

the charm around her neck and placed her attention on Gianna. Penny had planned to wait until after class, when she could go up to Gianna in person.

She had it all mapped out: Nayeli and Rose would say how brave she was for executing such a commanding performance, Gianna would give her one of those signature hugs, and the quad would eat lunch together every day and have sleepovers and maybe take a trip to Atlanta and all live happily ever after, the end. But Gianna's bizarre reaction to the reading made Penny second-guess herself. She couldn't risk not knowing what was really up. Her nose felt sparky, and she gripped her charm tighter. Gianna's thoughts echoed with the utmost clarity.

That was so embarrassing. Why did she have to do that? The last thing I wanted was for her to perform my poem. It's not hers; it's mine.

Penny's stomach twisted as if she'd just chugged rotten buttermilk. She dropped her charm and tucked it underneath her collar, and fastened the top button on her chambray shirt. The sensation of the icy Secrets Necklace against her bare skin sent a shiver down her spine, all the way to her toes.

The remaining ten minutes of class were torture.

Penny sneezed so many times that Max offered her some of the allergy lozenges he carried around on his person "at all times because the environment is unpredictable and crazy."

The moment the bell rang, Penny sprang out of her chair and over to Gianna.

"Hey," she said.

Gianna looked up and blinked sweetly, as if she hadn't been furious at Penny just minutes earlier.

"I'm . . . I didn't mean to—" Spark, spark, spark, spark, spark. Penny's eyes watered. Tingle, tingle, tingle. She blinked and held her breath. She couldn't sneeze now. She just couldn't. "I thought that—" Penny stopped short to hold her breath again. The more energy she spent squelching her sneeze, the more ferocious it became.

"Are you okay?" Gianna asked, appearing genuinely concerned. Penny frantically reached for her charm. Why had she buttoned her shirt up all the way to the top? That had been insane! Reckless! Catastrophic! Penny needed to listen in to what was really going on in Gianna's mind so she could fix this misunderstanding. Stupid chambray with its stupid buttons—what a steel trap of a garment! Penny scrambled to get her fingertips on her charm. Spark, spark, spark, spark, spark . . . *kapow!*

Penny sneezed so hard she was shocked her face didn't turn inside out.

"Bless you," Gianna said, not missing a beat.

Rose, who suddenly appeared by Gianna's side added, "You might need a tissue."

"They're on Mr. Turney's desk," Nayeli chimed in, still seated a few desks away, as if Penny couldn't have figured that out herself.

In case her face was covered in nightmarish post-sneeze goop, Penny skidded to Mr. Turney's desk for a tissue. It was the last one in the box. When she turned back around, Nayeli, Rose, and Gianna were gone.

"If you need a pass for the nurse, just let me know," Mr. Turney offered. "Allergies are a killer this time of year."

Penny nodded, humiliated, and packed up her things. She didn't have it in her to tell Mr. Turney that her "allergy" had nothing to do with the season and everything to do with her.

Chapter Fourteen

Six hours later Penny sat in her magnolia tree. Though sheltered from the world, she still couldn't escape the horrible feeling from poetry class.

Ever try to do something nice and it backfires in your face? she texted Otis. He was the only one she could sort of talk to. Or text to. Same difference.

Otis video called a moment later.

"Ghost Pepp!" he said when she pressed Accept. It was nice to hear his voice and see his face at the same time. It was so nice, Penny almost wanted to cry. Of course, she didn't. Instead, she joked.

"Dude," Penny greeted. "What's on your face?" Otis had grown a mustache. More like a mustache-lite. Penny could have counted the scrawny whiskers on one hand.

"The kitchen dudes are doing it. Whoever shaves theirs first loses."

"Might be worth taking the L on this one, dude," Penny teased.

"Ha-ha." Otis was a good sport. "If you fall out of that tree, Mom will kill me."

Penny rolled her eyes, but her heart made a little thump. It was a nice reminder that there was someone looking out for her. "Miss the magnolia?"

"Umm, yeah. My dumpy apartment complex doesn't have a single tree." Otis flipped his phone to show Penny the view out his window. Penny had to admit, it was pretty bleak. The mess of his bedroom didn't exactly add to the atmosphere.

"Pigsty, dude."

"Psh," Otis said. Before he spun the camera back around Penny caught him pulling up his blanket to give the semblance of a semi-made bed. "So what up?"

"Ohhh—" Penny stalled. Just seeing and hearing Otis made her feel better already. She didn't want to revisit that day's poetry nightmare. "Long story." Penny fiddled with the key-shaped charm around her neck. It had become habit. "Day off?" she diverted.

"Yup, yup," Otis said, stretching his arms overhead. "Gonna go grub it up on Buford Highway in a minute. Hit up a Malaysian spot, then tacos, and then bring it home with Korean BBQ." Buford Highway was a strip known for authentic (aka delicious) international food. Apparently. Penny had never been but she'd read about it on, like, a gazillion blogs. Best place in the Southeast for dumplings, pho, pupusas, curries, empanadas, banh mi, and more. No doubt about it, Buford Highway was Penny's fantasy dream house. Or fantasy dream highway. Whatever.

"Want to trade lives?"

"You don't, believe me. Not as great as it looks," Otis said with a smile, though for a split second Penny thought she heard a tinge of bitterness in his voice. "You're living the life," Otis joked. "Everyone in middle school following you around yet, or what?"

"Sure," Penny said quickly. She *really* did not want to talk about it.

"You're weirder than all of them put together, Ghost Pepp. And I mean that as a compliment."

"I know." Penny felt a tingle behind her eyeballs, which could mean only one thing, so she changed the subject. "What's the deal with friends and family, dude? I want to see you in action!"

"Umm, talking to Chef tomorrow I think." Otis looked away, as if someone was speaking to him from the other room, though Penny couldn't hear anyone else in the apartment. "Hey, I gotta go, my ride is here. Soon though, okay?"

"Ugh, you're so annoying," Penny fibbed. "Fine. Eat everything for me."

"That's a bet. Keep it weird, Ghost Pepp." Otis held his fist up to the camera for a virtual fist bump.

"Keepin' it weird," Penny said, gently tapping the screen with her own knuckles.

She stayed in the magnolia after the video chat ended, until the air had significantly cooled and the sun was down. Fireflies were officially gone for the season, so it was just Penny and the night. That magnolia tree was an essential element of a fantasy dream house. How had she forgotten to mention it the other day during the speed round? *Yes*, Penny thought, leaning her head back against the sturdy trunk, *Fantasy Dream House hall of fame material, no doubt about it.*

Penny stayed on the branch shaped like a bat wing until she heard her mom calling her in for a dinner that Penny, for the first time in weeks, hadn't prepared.

Penny used the energy she'd saved making dinner toward another PBttB attempt. She started with the same base recipe as the time before, but mixed in three room-temperature eggs instead of three right from the fridge. She also opened a fresh can of baking powder, just in case the one from last time was expired (there was no date on it, but she was pretty sure that it had been around for a while). On a whim, right before putting it in the oven, Penny sprinkled some sugar over the top of the batter.

That cake was the best one yet. Even Sylvia agreed.

Chapter Fifteen

Penny finally realized her mistake with Gianna. She just needed to really rely on her Secrets Necklace. Listen harder and longer. If she'd been more disciplined, she surely would have learned that Gianna wanted the spotlight for herself. Duh. She didn't even need the necklace to know that. Gianna was an aspiring Broadway actress. Duh, duh, duh.

So that's exactly what Penny Hoppe did. Like the good student she was (geometry excluded), she doubled down an all Secrets Necklace efforts.

Penny took the initiative to join the soccer girls at lunch on Monday. At first, she was a little annoyed they hadn't sought her out—Penny was stationed at her double-corner seat when she saw them arrive. But perhaps they hadn't seen her. She was in the corner, after all.

"Shooting practice on the books this afternoon, or what?"

"What book?" Reem asked, mouth full of macaroni and cheese.

"You know, ball-chaser extraordinaire, at your service!"

"Hah, oh yeah." Penny took Reem's acknowledgment as an invitation to sit.

The soccer girls picked up their conversation where they left off (some debate about if an under-the-sea theme was better than an outer-space theme), which was perfect, actually, because Penny was free to Secret Necklace to her heart's content.

But this time, listening in on the girls' thoughts didn't provide much she could work off of. Reem couldn't stop thinking about some guy named B.G. who she had a crush on, which was interesting for a second, but not exactly something Penny could ask about without revealing the origin of the query. After the theme debate came to an abrupt end, Shaylah's and Hollis's thoughts reflected their respect for geometry as a "math art," whatever that meant. As geometry was Penny's least favorite subject, she couldn't think of anything to contribute. Instead, she continued to absorb Reem's inner monologue about how long she needed to wait before texting B.G. back, which quickly became a snoozefest.

"Hello, Earth to Penny," Hollis said, waving her hand in front of Penny's face. "Are you here?"

"What?" Penny finally answered. It had taken her a moment to remember that when she heard Hollis's voice without that echo it meant she was speaking to her. In real life.

"Just making sure you're not sleeping with your eyes open."

Penny blinked.

"She's quiet," Reem said, by way of explanation.

"So what's with that necklace you always have on? Was it your grandma's or something? You said it was vintage, right?" Shaylah asked.

Penny snorted at the thought of Sylvia wearing anything so delicate. "It's just . . . a necklace." Penny hoped that explanation was sufficient.

"Can I try it on?" Shaylah said, already reaching behind Penny's neck for the clasp.

"No!" Penny said, jerking away.

"Jeez, calm down," Shaylah said, putting her hands up. *What, does it have magic powers or something?* Penny heard her think.

"No!" Penny exclaimed. "It does not have magic powers!" The sentence had just escaped her mouth when Penny realized what she'd done. She dropped her necklace and rushed both palms to her open mouth, as if to stuff the words back in.

Spark, tingle, spark, multiplied by a gazillion.

Shaylah and Hollis laughed. "Whoa, chill out," Hollis advised.

"Obviously it doesn't have magic powers," Shaylah replied. "Anyway, my bad." *What's with her?* Shaylah thought a second later. For a moment, Penny wished she could tell her the truth.

What a weird one, Penny heard Hollis think next. Penny was pretty sure Hollis hadn't meant the good kind of weird. Penny placed her attention on Reem, desperately hoping she'd have a kinder assessment of the interaction, but her mind was all B.G. and the hypothetical picnic he'd take her on as their first date. With the exception of two quick sneezes in succession, Penny kept quiet the rest of lunch.

Penny's next encounter with the Gang of Compounding Scientists wasn't much more rewarding. Not encounter. Near encounter.

The two sets of twins stood in the hallway between classes. Samson and Janiyah leaned against lockers, talking closely, while Sullivan and Jane bickered next to them about something or another.

Penny pretended to search for a pen in the bottom of her backpack a few feet away and listened. She wanted to share with them her most recent hall-of-fame Fantasy Dream House idea, but wasn't going to jump in before getting a sense of the inner monologue vibe. Just to make sure that Fantasy Dream House was still a thing.

Penny placed her attention on Samson and Janiyah first, ignoring their conversation, listening exclusively to their thoughts.

Are we flirting? I think we're flirting! Flirting is the best! Janiyah thought between giggles.

Janiyah is smart. Like, MIT smart. Whoa, Samson

thought, just as pretentious on the inside as on the outside.

They seemed too caught up in their low-key flirt to be bothered. No dice. Maybe there'd be an opening with Sullivan and Jane.

Again, the real-time arguing faded into muddled noise, and the duo's echoey thoughts took precedence.

Does Sullivan know that my ridiculous twin sister has a crush on his ridiculous twin brother?

Jane would be the worst sister-in-law.

Family squabbles at their seventh-grade peak. Penny didn't want to intrude. She zipped up her backpack and continued down the hall to her next class.

Where's she going? Penny heard Sullivan wonder right as she passed.

She was about to turn around—maybe Sullivan could be interested in her Fantasy Dream House idea after all—but she was careful to listen to Jane's thought first. She'd learned her lesson about being hasty and wasn't going to make that mistake again.

She's such a mystery, Jane thought. Spark, spark, major spark. Penny dashed to the bathroom to sneeze in private.

Chapter Sixteen

The day ended with art class. Penny's teacher, Ms. Citron, did that thing where she forced the class to sit in a new spot for no apparent reason. Penny ended up across from Lark, one table over from Gianna. Had the acoustics not been so poor in the art room she would have been within eavesdropping distance for sure.

Ms. Citron placed a small cactus, a swatch of velvet fabric, and an apple on a stool in the middle of the room to serve as a model for a still life. They had their choice of materials: paints, pencil, or pastels. Penny had opted for paints because they seemed the most forgiving. She'd been wrong. She'd only gotten to the cactus part of the painting but already it looked like a bag of spinach threw up another bag of spinach onto her paper. When she'd asked for a clean page to start fresh, Ms. Citron insisted she find a "creative solution." Ugh. Penny was convinced that most teachers had never actually been students themselves.

Penny stared at her catastrophe of a still life before dropping her brush in defeat. Across the table, Lark sat hunched over her sketch. Penny noticed that she used that same fine-tipped pen that she had in the cafeteria that day.

"How'd you get so good at drawing?" Penny asked.

Lark didn't answer. The way she gazed at her work in progress gave Penny the impression she saw something that Penny could not. Penny watched her for a bit before trying again.

"Hey."

Lark caught her breath, startled.

"Sorry," Penny backpedaled.

Lark jumped on the end of Penny's apology, explaining, "Sorry. I get super zoned in."

"I can tell," Penny said. "So, how did you learn how to draw like that?"

"Practice," Lark replied, eyes back on her work. Her voice was so soft Penny had to strain to hear. *The depth of the apple isn't right. Not right at all.* "The one that I did of New York is going to be in the newspaper."

"Really? I didn't know Lullwater Middle had a newspaper."

"No, the *Lullwater Chronicle*," Lark corrected. Her eyes remained on her task.

"That's so . . ." Penny searched for the right word. She found herself wanting to express herself just right when in Lark's presence. "Brave."

Lark stopped drawing and looked Penny in the eye. "Is it?"

"It's totally brave," Penny insisted. "I mean, what if people don't like it? Aren't you scared to let people see your work?" *Aren't you afraid to let people see you?* Penny thought.

"Nah. I like expressing myself with pictures. It's easier for me." Penny thought about that for a minute. She thought she understood. Maybe. "I dunno. It also relaxes me a lot," Lark revealed. "Don't you have anything like that?"

"Cooking," Penny blurted. "I love to cook. I learned from my brother, but I do it on my own now." Once she started talking, Penny couldn't stop. She told Lark all about Otis and how he'd moved to Atlanta to work in a restaurant's kitchen. Using a paintbrush, she demonstrated how to properly chop vegetables to reduce risk of finger decapitation. She described why making Everything-but-Meat Vegetable Soup was so fun to prepare, and that red wine vinegar was the secret ingredient because all good soups need a touch of acid. Lark continued to draw, but Penny could tell she was listening. It wasn't until the end of her monologue that Penny realized her hand had been on her Secrets Necklace the entire time, but she hadn't thought to use it once.

"Anyway, sorry to blab on and on. I guess you want to be an artist when you grow up and I want to be a chef."

Lark's face changed when she said that. But Penny didn't linger on her expression, because something else she heard caught her attention.

". . . for the bake sale?"

Penny looked at the table next to her where the voice—Gianna's voice—came from. She'd called out to Nayeli and Rose, who approached from the other end of the room.

"What do you think?" Gianna asked, holding up her painting for her friends (and anyone) to see. Well, it was a painting, technically, but it was also a sign. "Mr. Turney said if we wanted color copies I had to give him the original by the end of school today."

"Awesome," Nayeli said.

"Perfecto!" Rose exclaimed.

In expressive, loopy Gianna lettering, the sign read, *Support your local thespians! Bake sale Thursday! After school in the Cavern! Get your sweet tooth on!* Beneath the text she'd drawn a delicious-looking cupcake covered in multi-colored sprinkles, and the classic comedy and tragedy theater masks. It was an incredibly eye-catching poster.

They continued to excitedly chatter about bake sale plans, the volume of their conversation rising above all competing sounds. Quickly, Penny dropped the paintbrush slash kitchen knife in her hand and reached for her charm. She heard Gianna's echoey thought loud and clear:

I hope we have enough cookies. I'm not sure Nayeli and Rose will pull their weight.

It couldn't be more perfect.

Lark still had that curious look on her face a moment later when class ended, but Penny didn't bother to think more about it. Penny quickly cleaned up her materials and darted out the door. She had a lot of baking to do.

Chapter Seventeen

At first, Penny had debated what kind of cookie to make. Her famous Peanut Butter Lover cookies were what immediately came to mind, but then she second-guessed that choice. Otis loved the kick of nutmeg, but what if that wasn't a universal taste? Penny should have Secret Necklaced Gianna longer to determine what kind of cookie she preferred. In the end, she played it safe and just went with a standard sugar cookie. Topped with rainbow sprinkles, of course, to match Gianna's poster.

In the middle of her baking extravaganza, Penny remembered to text Otis. He'd have had his meeting with the chef by now. Penny was annoyed for a second that he hadn't told her about it, but quickly read between the silent lines. Promotion! Otis was too busy to text because he worked nights on the line now! Penny wiped the flour off her hands and furiously typed into her phone.

1. How was Buford?

2. You better take me on a food tour when I come visit.

3. Just because you're officially a fancy line cook doesn't mean you're too cool to talk to me now.

Hello? Is my fancy line cook brother too cool to talk to me now?

Seriously, how's the kitchen? When can we come see you in action now that you're an official LINE COOK?

Hours later, when Penny was elbow-deep asleep, Otis responded. Sry. Busy.

The morning of the bake sale, Penny woke up before dawn to encase each individual cookie in plastic wrap (food service film was what they called it in the industry). Penny'd done the math. She knew there were five hundred students at Lullwater Middle School, give or take. That was about twenty batches of two dozen cookies. Penny wasn't a fool. She knew not everybody would come to the bake sale. So she'd made ten batches—a total of two hundred and forty cookies—and called it a day. Or two sleepless nights. Whatever.

"You're still not finished with those cookies?" Dad said with a yawn as he stumbled into the kitchen to turn on the coffeepot.

"I told you, Dad, I had to make a lot," Penny snapped.

"Hey, just asking," Dad said. "So this is for your friend's bake sale?"

"Yup," Penny answered. Food service film was such an annoying way to wrap cookies. There had to be a better way. Next time she could try parchment paper . . . though that presented a host of other problems.

"Well, they're certainly lucky to have you," he said, giving Penny a pat on the head as he stole a cookie from the unwrapped pile.

"Hey!"

"Mmm, that is the best darn thing—" He paused to stuff the rest in his mouth. Dessert for breakfast. It ran in the family. "You give me a shout when the coffee's done. I'm gonna close my eyes for . . . seven more minutes," he said. Dad was champion of the snooze button. Drove Mom crazy. Penny was surprised he'd even made it down to turn on the coffee.

"Yup, yup," Penny chimed.

Penny grinned and continued wrapping. If she kept pace, she'd be done in time to whip up some soft scrambled eggs for breakfast.

Two hundred forty cookies were heavy. No way around it. They hardly fit in Penny's locker, where she'd stashed them for the day. Carrying them through a bustling hallway after school en route to the Cavern did not make for easy transport. Penny was out of breath by the time she arrived outside the school's front doors.

The sale was already set up. Gianna and company had hung a big banner that was basically a larger version of the poster. Despite the jazzy presentation, Gianna, Rose, and Nayeli looked a bit lonely behind their table of store-bought baked goods; customers were scarce. Penny proceeded with confidence. Her homemade cookies were going to get the sale going, without a doubt.

"I made these for the bake sale," Penny said, the

two canvas grocery bags full of treats weighing down her shoulders. "There should be enough for . . . everyone, pretty much!"

"Whoa, you did?" Gianna asked, clearly impressed. Or stunned. Or both.

Penny nodded. And smiled. She was proud of her hard, delicious work.

"Holy moly," Nayeli exclaimed.

Penny placed one bag of cookies on the table and one underneath.

"Well, enjoy!" Penny said, and turned to go.

"Hey, stay and hang out," Gianna offered. "Don't you want to see everyone enjoy your hard work?"

Huh. The thought had never occurred to Penny before. Determined not to repeat her prior mistakes, Penny rapidly enclosed her hand around her charm, and paused to listen. *I had no idea she was such a good baker.* Penny pepped up with that news. Then, *But I hope she knows she doesn't have to do all that to hang with us.*

Ping. Gianna's words—err, thoughts—hit Penny's chest like a small poison dart.

"Umm," Penny stammered. "Actually, I'm kind of beat." She faked a yawn that quickly turned into a real one. And then morphed into a sneeze. Penny didn't know a sneeze-yawn combo platter was even possible.

"She's so mysterious," Penny heard Nayeli whisper to Rose and Gianna.

Penny ignored her homework when she got home. Instead, she went straight to the kitchen. Sylvia sat alert at the kitchen table, *Honestly, Jacques* in her hands. Her lips moved as she read, as if tasting the words.

"Don't mind me," Penny sneered.

"Mhmm," Sylvia offered in way of response. She only had a handful of pages left in her book.

All the mixing bowls, measuring cups, and baking sheets were still on the dish rack. It took all of Penny's control not to throw them to the ground. The crash they'd make might have been satisfying. But no matter how upset she was, Penny knew ruining perfectly good kitchenware would not change the fact that she was the weirdest-in-the-wrong-way seventh grader who ever walked the earth, and who would never make any friends her own age no matter how hard she tried.

That was the second time someone had called her "mysterious." Penny didn't get it. She was a nervous weirdo (in a good way but maybe also in a not-so-good way); anyone could see that. If she didn't wear those flaws so obviously on her sleeve, Penny would have no reason to sneeze.

Penny was halfway into Garbage Dump Chili when Mom entered the kitchen. Her headphones hung around her neck. She usually wasn't home this early.

"You don't have to make dinner every night, Penny girl."

Penny ignored her, and continued stirring the onions. They were starting to smell delicious. Just another thirty seconds or so until they'd turn translucent; then it would be time to add the green peppers and garlic.

"Really," Mom said. She walked over to the stove and took a big inhale. "Mmm. I do love your chili, but you can take a night off."

Penny knew it wasn't nice, but she couldn't help but roll her eyes. A night off? Mom sure wasn't one to talk. Penny couldn't remember the last time she'd seen her mother farther than eavesdropping distance of her headset.

Penny shoveled a pile of diced green peppers and a few cloves of finely chopped garlic from the cutting board into the pot. They sizzled in the heat. Penny gave the concoction another stir.

"Or, you could invite your friends over for dinner. I'd even help you cook!"

What planet was Mom on? Penny dropped the wooden spoon in her hand and turned to face her mother.

"Mom. I like to cook. That's my *thing*. What is your problem?" Penny had never really spoken to her mom like that before. The words felt sticky and sour coming out of her mouth. Still, she continued. "What is the big deal about friends?"

"Don't take that tone with me," Mom snapped back. And then, softer, "I know it's been hard for you since Otis left—"

"I'm fine. I'm very, very fine. More than fine. Fine," Penny added for good measure. Her cheeks were hot. Ghost-pepper hot. Penny reached for her charm. Despite its frigid surface, it did little to cool Penny's temperature or anger.

Mom opened her mouth to respond, but her phone rang. She hesitated, looked at the number of the incoming call, and sighed. She was more tired than angry, it seemed. "I'm not done with you," Mom warned, before she marched upstairs. "Thank you for calling O&P Temperatures, this is Mollie, how may I help you . . ."

Penny took a deep breath. Because that's what you were supposed to do after screaming at your mom when she was only trying to help, right? A bitter scent invaded her nose. Burned garlic. The saddest, most regretful smell Penny knew.

Penny rushed to the stove. The tiny bits of garlic were crisped to a dark black and stuck to the rim of the pot. The chili was destroyed. She carried the pot to the sink and turned on the faucet. Steam exploded as the water made contact with the heated aluminum.

"Am I really that mysterious?" she mumbled, waiting for the pot to cool.

"Only because you want to be," Sylvia said, without missing a beat. Penny wasn't sure if she was quoting her book or answering her question.

Penny shut off the water and shuffled into the living room. The lizards were often active in the late afternoon. Pet lizards counted as friends, right?

Penny had botched dinners before. Ingredients burned, pots boiled over. It happened. This was the first time she didn't quite have the gumption to start again.

That night they had delivery pizza for dinner. Mom was on an emergency call that lasted for hours. Penny, Dad, and Sylvia ate in silence, with the exception of the moments Sylvia complained that the cheese on the pie was too "melty." Whatever that meant. Penny fed her crusts to the lizards.

Yes, cooking was Penny's thing. What was so mysterious about that? Why didn't Mom get it? Cooking was Penny's thing. It was Otis's thing. It was *their* thing. It was what she loved and what she was good at. Hanging out with other people was overrated. Right? Right.

Chapter Eighteen

"Penny girl, get over here," Dad called from the living room that Saturday morning. Late morning. Two minutes before afternoon, technically.

Penny was still in bed. And had no intentions of getting up anytime soon. Especially for Dad to show her something "amazing" that Millions, Rent, or (probably not) Scraffy had done. Dad's announcements were usually lizard-gymnastics related. But Penny hadn't officially made up with Mom since their fight, so she suspected she was in for . . . something. She just didn't know what.

When Penny emerged in the living room, pjs wrinkled and eyes puffy, Mom and Dad didn't waste any time.

"Get dressed. We're going to Atlanta."

* * *

They arrived at Aujourd'hui late afternoon, right when dinner service began. They'd stopped to go apple picking (a totally overrated activity, in Penny's opinion); Mom and Dad couldn't resist a fresh Granny Smith. Despite nibbling on their harvest in the backseat, Penny was starving when they arrived. And excited. They couldn't get a reservation because of the last-minute nature of the visit ("We're due in for a little fun," Mom explained when Penny asked about the occasion for such a treat. "Plus, summer was good to O&P."), but over the phone the maître d' said they'd have a good shot at a prime table by the kitchen if they showed up right at 5 p.m. When Mom, Dad, and Penny stepped through the doors at 5:07 p.m., the dining room was nearly empty.

Aujourd'hui was like no restaurant Penny had ever seen. Otis had described it as a "white tablecloth, tweezer food kinda place" (whatever that meant), but there wasn't a white tablecloth in sight. The restaurant actually reminded Penny of an extremely luxurious barn. The ceilings were very high, exposed rafters adding to the grandeur. The elegant tables were all made of impeccably polished wood. And the chairs! Nothing like the ones at Penny's house. They were covered in fabric, like individual couches! To sit on while eating! Rustic wooden planks decorated the two walls with the giant floor-to-ceiling windows. The wall surrounding the open kitchen was covered with shiny white rectangular tiles, providing a spotlight of sorts on the culinary action. A long steel counter made up the pass (the area where cooks placed dishes ready to be picked up and served), and low-hanging lights providing ample glow for the plates to come.

But it wasn't the pass that most interested Penny—it was everything behind: the kitchen. A gigantic stove *and* a grill over a live wood fire. Dozens of sauté pans hanging from overhead hooks. Miles and miles of prep space. Stacks and stacks of white plates. A giant stockpot bubbled next to what appeared to be a fryer. Every cooking station was equipped with squeeze bottles and plastic quart containers. The expeditor (the kitchen conductor, essentially) called, "Fire mains for forty-one" (aka start cooking the main dishes for table forty-one). The kitchen reminded Penny of a machine; everybody had a job and a place. Nobody was left out, every action essential.

Penny took the seat with the direct view of the

kitchen. She was so amped she could barely maintain a conversation with her parents, who mostly just marveled about the decor. Mom didn't mention their little tiff, so Penny assumed the whole thing had blown over. Her parents, she noted, were happy. Delighted, actually. Perhaps a little mini day trip down to the city was exactly what all the Hoppes needed.

Penny didn't see Otis behind the pass right away. Though, at first it was difficult to tell. All of the cooks wore matching white caps and white smock shirt things, which seemed silly considering cooking was a very spill-splatter-stain-friendly business.

A server with a crisp white button-up shirt tucked into a denim apron with leather straps approached their table. Her curly blond hair was tied back in a low ponytail, and her bright red lipstick was perfectly within the lip lines. "Can I offer you complimentary sparkling or flat?"

"Water?" Dad said.

"Duh, it's water," Penny hissed. "Sparkling for me, please!"

"Sure. Sparkling all around," Mom confirmed.

"Is this your first time dining with us?"

"Yes," Penny answered for the three of them.

"Fabulous. Welcome. So a little bit about Aujourd'hui: Chef Jacques believes that all food expresses a sense of place. Everything you see on the menu has been locally sourced within thirty miles of the restaurant. We do curate our menu daily and all our dishes are intended to share. In addition to what you see on the menu, we also have butter bean mousse; a foraged salad with nettles, pistachio dust, and edible flowers; and a Piedmontese Ax steak, bone-in, at three dollars an ounce."

"I don't know what those things are," Dad whispered, a little too loud for Penny's comfort.

Penny rolled her eyes, though, if she were being honest, of the dishes mentioned, only several of the ingredients involved rang a bell. Penny guessed a *nettle* was either in the pinecone or tea kettle family.

"Do you have truffles available?" Penny asked.

The server laughed before she saw Penny was serious. "As truffles aren't harvested within the immediate region, we do not serve them here at Aujourd'hui."

"Oh," Penny said, doing her best to conceal her disappointment.

"I'll be right back with your water."

"Wait, what station is Otis working?" Penny asked.

She craned her neck to get a different view of the kitchen, but he was nowhere in sight. Maybe he was on break or finishing up the last scraps of family meal. Otis always went in for seconds . . . and thirds . . . and sometimes fourths if they were available.

The server looked back at the kitchen before answering. "Otis . . . he's in the back tonight, I think."

Huh. That was weird. He should be working cold apps. Maybe because it was still slow he was helping with prep? That made sense. "Thanks," Penny replied. Then added, "And don't tell him I asked."

The server walked away, vanishing behind the bar.

Penny turned to her parents. She held her key-shaped charm and twirled the chain around her finger. "So he has no idea we're here?"

"Nope," Mom said. The last rays of sun beamed in through the window. Her gold hoop earrings shimmered in the light. Mom always wore hoops for occasions. Mom looked much more awake without her headset, Penny realized.

"We thought we'd go for the double surprise: first you, then Oatmeal," Dad explained. Otis hated that nickname, but Dad wouldn't give it up for anything.

How are we going to surprise him if he's in the back? Penny wondered.

The server returned with sparkling water and took their order. Mom and Dad said to live it up, ("Record-breaking radiator emergencies this month—business has been good!" they explained to the server, who nodded politely), so Penny picked a handful of dishes for the table. Their appetizers (heirloom lettuce that came with a free-range soybean oil vinaigrette, three espresso cups of bone broth, and local bee pollen on spelt crackers) arrived ten minutes later, and still no sign of Otis.

"I have to text him," Penny said after she'd taken a surprisingly satisfying slurp of broth.

Penny took a photo of the salad, and then another of the kitchen, and sent them to her brother.

"Are you sure he's working tonight?" Penny confirmed.

"That's what he said," Mom answered.

The main course had been cleared from the table when Otis finally emerged. He wore black-and-white-checkered pants, black clogs, and a red bandanna underneath the standard white cap. His mustache, unfortunately, looked more pathetic in person. And he slumped a little more than Penny remembered. Penny was short for her age, and somehow, Otis had always been very tall. It gave Penny hope that she had a spurt coming. But most of all, Penny noticed that he looked tired and, despite the lackluster facial hair, a bit older than the last time she saw him. He gave them all hugs but didn't seem all that excited *or* surprised. *Probably playing it cool*, Penny thought. He stood next to the table, back to the kitchen, towering over his family.

"So far so, so good!" Penny praised. She wasn't lying. The food was not bad. It was not her cup of tea—err, bone broth—but it was definitely tasty and interesting, two valuable qualities in a meal. "What did you make?"

Before Otis could answer, their server appeared. She held a very large and very shallow bowl with a small amount of . . . something . . . in the center. A dollop of chocolate ice cream? Unclear. "Compliments of the kitchen." She smiled and placed the bowl, along with three spoons, down on the table. "Pecan semifreddo infused with Georgia red clay essence."

"Is this yours?" Penny asked.

"Umm, nope," Otis said curtly. Had she said something wrong? Would her Secrets Necklace work on him? He wasn't *not* her peer, right?

Penny took a bite of the semifreddo (not bad, but not Bendy's, and also not exactly ice cream, either) and held the charm between her fingertips. Nothing. The charm felt colder on her skin than the semi-whatever did on her tongue.

Secretly, Penny had planned to ask Otis for a tour of the kitchen. It would probably break some sort of health code, but it was worth a shot. Otis slipped away to the hidden part of the kitchen right after the dessert arrived, so she never got the chance.

Otis was being a weirdo. And Penny did not mean that as a compliment.

"Dude, why are you sucking so much tonight?" Penny accused when she met Otis around back. After dessert she'd texted in all caps, WHAT IS WRONG WITH YOU? Immediately, he'd instructed her to meet him around the back of the restaurant in the break area. Tell Mom and Dad it's well-lit and safe, he added, anticipating their protests. Penny suggested her parents order coffee and excused herself from the table, half explaining her destination. They did not argue, though Mom said if she wasn't back in ten minutes she would make a scene.

The break area was basically a spot of asphalt outside the back entrance of the restaurant, designated by the presence of several plastic milk crates strewn about. Otis was leaning against the brick wall next to the steel door when Penny walked up.

"Why'd you guys even come? I said I'd tell you when I could get friends and family," Otis said.

"I dunno. Mom and Dad said they signed some new big contract doing heat at a country club, so I guess they wanted to splurge? What's the big deal? We all thought you'd be excited to see us!"

I was excited to see you, Penny thought.

"I just—" Otis stopped, as if he didn't know how to say what he meant. "I wasn't ready for y'all to see me here yet. It's not quite like I made it out to be. Obviously."

Otis explained that maybe he'd exaggerated a bit. He was still on day prep half the time, and his only night shifts were washing dishes. Which was why

Penny hadn't seen him cooking on the line in the visible part of the kitchen. Sure, he was learning a lot about technique but the vibe was also formal and strange and so not his style. The chef was a pompous lunatic who screamed all the time, which was "industry standard" (whatever that meant), but also made the simplest tasks like chopping potatoes very stressful. Otis spent a lot of energy trying not to make a mistake.

When his confession was over, Otis sighed and sat down on a milk crate. Penny lowered herself to the one next to him. She didn't quite know what to say.

"You know why I like to cook, Penny?"

He called her Penny. He must be serious.

"Because chopping and mixing stuff is fun and relaxing?" That's why Penny liked to cook.

"Sure. But that's not it." Otis paused. "This sounds cheesy, I know, and if you tell Chef, I'll pee in the batter the next time I make you pancakes, but it's because it connects me to people in a way. It's hard to do that with words for me. You know that." Penny did, she realized. She thought back to all of Otis's spotty texts. The short answers, the jokes instead of sentiments, and the quick goodbye before he'd jumped into his loaded car and driven away from their little yellow house on Plum Street. All of that made a lot more sense now. "Cooking is something I've always been good at. It made up for the stuff I'm not so good at, in a way. But I don't feel like that now. Not anymore. I think I'm in over my head."

"What are you talking about? You're literally the best cook I know."

Otis scoffed. "That has nothing to do with anything."

Penny didn't see how that could be true, but she kept quiet.

"Chef won't give me the time of day. He'd fire me before he'd promote me."

"Did he say that?" Penny asked, eyes wide. This chef sounded like a real piece of work. She'd like to tell him a thing or two.

"No."

"Then how do you know?"

"I can just tell. He probably thinks I'm just some loser kid from the boonies." If Otis was some loser kid from the boonies, what did that make her? Penny pushed the thought out of her head. Then, after a long silence, Otis admitted, "Maybe I am. I've almost quit and come home so many times."

That took Penny's breath away. She blurted, "What? You can't do that!"

Nothing had been the same since Otis left, and she missed him every day. But quitting Aujourd'hui? Coming back home just because some "big shot" chef was scary? No. That wasn't right. Not at all. Penny furrowed her brow, thinking it all through. She couldn't quite find the words to express herself. Maybe that quality did run in the family.

"You too busy now with all your new friends? Don't want me invading your social life, huh?" Otis's joke fell flat. Neither sibling was quite ready for a laugh. Otis shivered, rubbed the goose bumps off his arms, and stood to stretch. Penny ran hot and her brother ran cold. "I love to cook. I love making food other people can enjoy. It's how I share who I am. And yes, I know that was super corny, too, so I'll stop right there." Penny didn't think it sounded corny at all, but Otis seemed to have his mind made up. He dropped his hands by his side. "Anyway, I just miss all that. The part of cooking that I love. And washing dishes sure ain't it."

"What about Project Better than the Box?"

"What about it?" Penny felt a little ping in her chest; Otis's words seared.

"That's not washing dishes. You gave up on it already?"

"No, Penn, I just don't have time. The oven in my apartment hardly works and I don't want to get in Chef's way here," Otis said, pointing inside. "Speaking of, I gotta go back in."

Penny stood and did her best to hide her disappointment. Her disappointment about so many things, most of which she couldn't even name.

"Yeah. Me too." Penny consulted the time on her phone. Ten minutes wasn't even up yet. "I guess I'll go rescue our server. Mom and Dad are probably telling her why they named O&P Temperatures 'O&P Temperatures.'"

"'Cause one baby ran hot and one baby ran cold," the siblings said in unison, though the punch line lacked their usual spunk.

"Keep it weird, Ghost Pepp," Otis said, holding out his fist.

"Yeah," Penny mumbled, meeting his knuckles with her own.

Otis opened the door to the kitchen. Bright light and some horrific heavy metal music spilled out into the night. A moment later the door shut and he was gone. Penny felt tears well as she walked back to meet her parents, but she didn't dare let one fall.

Chapter Nineteen

The auditorium was different when it was empty. Bigger. Taller. Penny, along with the rest of her class, sat in the first couple rows while Ms. Samich explained what was to come.

"Welcome to dress rehearsal," Ms. Samich chimed once the class had settled. Behind her, the stage was vacant except for a microphone on a stand.

"So at the final performance next week, you will all wait in line backstage and then come out one by one. Today, for the dress rehearsal, I just want you all to get comfortable with the space and using the microphone." Ms. Samich gave a thumbs-up to Mr. Turney, who looked like he was ready for a nap. Or a maybe winter hibernation.

The class was antsy. In order to accommodate the auditorium schedule, their class had been moved to fourth period, right before lunch. Fourth period was always a disaster. Everybody was hungry and nobody was in any mood to be educated, Penny included. Penny sat between Mateo and Janiyah. Out of habit, Penny employed her Secrets Necklace for a quick listen. Mateo was still anxious about his voice cracking (now that she looked, he was low-key massaging his vocal cords) and Janiyah missed Jane (apparently Jane was giving her twin the cold shoulder now that Janiyah and Samson were officially crushing on each other). Gianna sat at the other end of the row, just out of eavesdropping distance. She'd be up third.

Penny had been sneezing all day. More than usual, even. She couldn't shake the whole conversation she'd had with Otis outside of Aujourd'hui. He felt far away in a way he never had before. Just thinking about it set off sparks.

To make matters worse, Penny couldn't find her poetry journal anywhere. She'd torn apart her entire bedroom, locker, and book bag. She'd even looked in all the kitchen cabinets, pantry, and, in a moment of real desperation, the lizard tank. No luck. Penny was not forgetful; losing something with such treasured contents was just not like her. Penny was beginning to think it had evaporated. Which would have actually been the most ideal option because that meant it wasn't floating around in public for anyone and everyone to see, read, judge, ridicule, and/or upload onto the internet.

Tingle, tingle, spark, spark.

When Gianna took her turn onstage, Penny couldn't even look at her. She was still so ashamed about how she'd embarrassed Gianna when reading her work in class. Plus, what she'd overheard her think at the bake sale still stung.

Tingle, spark, tingle, spark.

Otis couldn't quit and come home. Just the thought of that made Penny sick. She'd love to see him more, but that just didn't seem right. Next bake sale she'd only make two dozen cookies. Or maybe none and all! How would Gianna like that?

"Penny H.!" Ms. Samich's voice snapped Penny out of her spiraling daydream. "You're up."

Penny looked to her right and saw the seat was empty. Sure enough Mateo shuffled down from the stage. By the looks of it, his voice had definitely cracked while reading his poem. Perhaps more than once.

Penny stood and walked toward the stage, thankful her seat was only one in from the aisle so she didn't have to squirm over too many legs. At least one good thing had come from reading Gianna's poem in class: Penny wasn't too nervous to get onstage. She took the copy of her poem out of her pocket. Penny had started and finished her backup non-personal "Where I'm From" poem on a loose piece of paper, so she couldn't have read her beautiful, private, and heart-felt work even if she had wanted to. Which she for sure, no doubt about it, absolutely did not want to do.

Penny ascended the stairs to the stage and approached the mic. She'd never set foot on that stage before. On any stage, now that she thought about it. The room appeared even larger from her viewpoint. Way too much space for a small girl with unruly bangs to fill.

Tingle. Just a small one. But still, a tingle.

"Hi, I'm Penny Hoppe," Penny said. She stood on her tiptoes. The mic was too tall. Adjusting it lower seemed hard. And risky. She didn't even know how. She noticed some movement in the audience. T.C. whispered something to Theo and they cracked up. Ryder kicked the back of the chair in front of him, which happened to be Jane's seat. She said nothing. Max looked like he was plotting a murder mystery, and Cole was obviously flexing all of his upper body muscles at once.

Mini spark.

Penny clutched her charm. Just a quick check-in. To pump her up, like last time she read, in class.

Dress rehearsals are for amateurs, Max thought.

Hate. Everything. About. School, she heard Ryder think.

Why is she taking so long? Cole thought.

Penny cleared her throat.

"'Where I'm From,'" she said grandly, motioning her arm that held the paper out to the left. Too grandly. And too loud. An ear-piercing sound came from the speakers. Nayeli and Rose covered their ears. Shocked by the volume she was able to create, Penny jumped back.

What's the point of dress rehearsal? Nayeli thought.

So bored, Rose thought.

Penny gulped. She wasn't entertaining them at all. She thought about backing out but—no. She'd done that before. Not again. She just needed a small bit of positive reinforcement. She scanned the crowd and—surprise, surprise—her eyes landed on Gianna. She sat attentively, as she always did, a light smile gracing her face.

"Whenever you're ready, Penny H.," Ms. Samich encouraged. "Take a deep breath if you need to. I know it can be intimidating up there."

If only she knew the half of it. Ms. Samich still had so, so much to learn.

But Penny took the big breath anyway and placed her attention squarely on Gianna. She clenched her necklace. The teeth on the end of the key imprinted against the fleshy insides of her fingers. Penny exhaled and listened.

I wish I knew more about her. She's so—

And then suddenly, Gianna's echoey voice went silent. Penny gripped her necklace tighter. She took another inhale, stared straight at Gianna, and listened again.

Nothing.

Explosive spark. Record-breaking tingle.

Her peers in the audience rustled. Penny couldn't stall any longer without encouraging a pre-lunch revolt. She blinked one last time and spit out the first line of the safe, alternate version of her poem.

"I'm from Lullwater, Georgia. Born and raised."

Penny paused after the first line and tried her Secrets Necklace again. Maybe it just wasn't working on Gianna. She placed her attention on Janiyah, who whispered quietly to Samson in the second row. They were making fun of her, Penny knew it. Obviously. Penny held the charm with all her might.

Nothing.

"I'm from blond bangs and shorter-than-average height."

What was going on? She needed her charm to work. And fast! T.C. and Theo joined Ryder in kicking the seats in front of them. Max was blatantly asleep now, a scowl plastered to his face. Mateo rolled his eyes. Gianna yawned, politely covering her mouth with her hand.

Penny tugged at her charm, willing it to work. The irregular shape felt like a whole vanilla bean inside her clammy fist. Maybe if she just squeezed it as tight as possible it would . . .

Pop.

The chain snapped, free-falling from around her neck. The charm remained in her hand while the chain dangled between her fingers. Penny stared at the broken necklace in disbelief.

"I'm from a house with my mom and dad and step-grandma thank you the end."

Penny didn't wait for applause. She didn't take a bow. She didn't look a single classmate in the eye. She just sparked and tingled her way back to her seat, where she shoved the broken necklace deep into her pocket. For the remaining fifteen minutes of class Penny kept her hand clenched around the charm. When she finally released her grip as she filed out of the auditorium at the end of the dress rehearsal, she saw that the stone on the key-shaped charm was no longer a deep blue. Like a radioactive cyclone, the stone swirled a fluorescent tie-dye.

Chapter Twenty

Penny left school at lunch. She just couldn't take it anymore. Getting a sick note from the nurse wasn't hard. She couldn't stop sneezing.

"I'm home because I'm sick," Penny announced as she walked through the front door of the little yellow house on Plum Street. Since she'd been old enough to walk to and from school, she'd never come home early for any reason. Penny went straight to the kitchen and was not surprised to see Sylvia posted up at her usual spot at the table. She appeared to be writing a letter in the most elegant cursive, not the same block letters she used for crossword puzzles. Her beloved book rested on the table next to her, cover side up.

"Wash your hands," Sylvia said by way of acknowledgment.

Penny did as she was told. Not because of sick

germs but because she planned to make something to eat, and hand washing before food handling was a must. Obviously. Kitchen basics 101.

A moment later Mom emerged, headset around her neck, gigantic contractor bag full of clothes in her arms. Sometimes she took calls from home so she could "double-task."

"You okay, Penny girl?" she asked, immediately pressing the back of her hand to Penny's forehead, as if a fever was the only thing that counted as "sick."

Penny sniffled. Leftover from all the sparks and tingles that morning. Nothing more.

"Yes, I think. Going to make a sick snack," Penny explained.

Mom gave her a look. She knew that look. Mom saw right through her. Penny braced herself to be scolded, but instead Mom pulled her in for a hug. "A new jar of grape jelly is in the pantry. Don't use the one in the fridge; I think it's older than Sylvia. I'd fix it for you, but I know you'd rather do it yourself." Mom was right. "I'm in my room sorting donations. An extra haul to Tina's this weekend with winter clothes. Come in if you need anything. Or run out of jelly."

Penny nodded.

"Keep an eye on her, Syliva," Mom ordered.

Sylvia grunted, and continued writing.

Penny padded to the pantry to get the ingredients. "Sick snack" was an old family recipe. Mom's mom made it for her when she was a kid. Simple, but extremely effective. Store-brand grape jelly on sandwich crackers. The jelly had to be purple, and the crackers had to be square, but otherwise that was it.

"What is the purpose of the Secrets Necklace anyway if it is just going to break on me when I needed it most?" Penny muttered to herself as she placed the jelly on the counter and tore into a new sleeve of crackers. "Knife and paper towel." Penny took a knife from the utensil drawers. Another thing about sick snack: It was optimally served on a paper towel, not a plate.

"Mhmm," Sylvia hummed.

Penny opened the jar of jelly and began spreading. She continued to narrate her own work. "Not too thick, but not too thin. It's a bad recipe, if you ask me. What's the point of knowing others' secrets? And what is so mysterious about *me*, anyway?"

"Mhmmm."

Penny brushed her bangs out of her eyes with her forearm.

"The stupid necklace didn't even help me. I heard dozens—actually more like hundreds—of kids' thoughts. All that info taken and for what purpose? I'm still buddy-less, still sneezing nonstop. *Finito*." Penny dropped the sticky knife in the sink and screwed the top on the jelly. She'd leave that and the crackers out in case she wanted more later. Sick snacks were addictive.

Penny was about to carry her napkin of jelly crackers to her room, when she spotted the container of rainbow sprinkles left over from her bake sale extravaganza. Impulsively, she unscrewed the cap and gave the bottle a quick shake. A flurry of multi-colored sprinkles flurried onto the gelatinous purple jelly.

"Sometimes recipes are meant to be broken," Sylvia said, not looking up. Penny had forgotten she was even there.

"You're mixing that up with another saying, Sylvia," Penny said.

"You heard me right. Broken recipes are the secret ingredient."

Penny thought about that for a few seconds before shaking her head. The phrase made her brain feel as if it had pulled a muscle. It had been a long day. A long few weeks. A long seventh grade, and it wasn't even a quarter over. Talk about mysterious; Sylvia could have written the book.

"Okay, Sylvia, whatever you say."

Penny carried her sick snack with her into the comfort of her own bedroom.

Penny closed the door behind her (because privacy, duh) and retrieved her recipe box from under her bed. She hadn't thought to look at it in a while. Maybe she'd forgotten a step, a few lines of even finer print, or instructions for Secrets Necklace reactivation.

Penny took the broken Secrets Necklace out of her pocket and placed it on her bedspread. It was still curiously warm to the touch, though the color of the stone had transformed to a dull, lifeless black. She opened the wooden box and picked up the first recipe card in the stack. The writing caught her by surprise.

Instead of a cheeky "recipe" for a magic necklace, all Penny found were alarmingly simple instructions for fruit salad.

RECIPE NAME: FRIVOLOUS FRUIT SALAD

Ingredients:
Your favorite fruits! Every single one!

Directions:
    Preparation time: 10 minutes
    Step 1: Cut fruits into bite-size pieces.
    Step 2: Combine all in a large bowl.
    Step 3: Enjoy!

Ick. Penny didn't even like fruit salad. It was a reckless and undisciplined dish, in her opinion. Disappointed, Penny dropped her broken necklace into the box and slammed it shut. Penny Hoppe no longer had a recipe to follow.

Hopeless, but still hungry, Penny wanted more crackers and jelly. When she opened the door to her room to head back to the kitchen, she ran smack into Mom.

"Oh sorry, Penny girl, I was just about to knock." _Sure_, Penny thought. Mom had Penny's winter jacket in hand. The subtle syrup stain on the sleeve was still there from the time she and Otis tried to eat pancakes in the magnolia tree Christmas morning two years ago. "Do you think this still fits you?"

Probably, Penny thought. She remained tiny for her age.

Mom held up the jacket in front of Penny. "Yeah, it's a little small, I think." It looked fine to Penny. "Are you okay if I bring it to Tina's for the coat drive and we get you a new one?"

Penny shrugged.

"I'll take that as a yes. You need something you can grow into."

Penny nodded, though a part of her was afraid she might never grow at all.

Chapter twenty-One

The next day at school, things were already back to the way they'd always been pre–Secrets Necklace. Except they were also different. Though Penny wasn't collecting new information, she hadn't forgotten the things she'd learned about her peers when the Secrets Necklace was fully functional.

A few days post–Secrets Necklace deactivation, Penny saw Max sitting at a separate table from T.C. and Theo at lunch. She felt bad for him. Max put on a brave face but Penny suspected, based on the thoughts she'd heard and the surreptitious glances he continued to give T.C. and Theo, that he felt left out. Instead of eating alone in her corner, Penny sat down across from him.

"So tell me about camp. Is it really true you don't have a curfew if you're a junior counselor?"

"How did you know I was a counselor?" Max asked, still gazing at his friends.

"Lucky guess," Penny fibbed. "So what's it like?"

"Well, honestly, it's the best." Max, like an open faucet, proceeded to tell her all about his summer; the nights they'd snuck out, the adorable nine-year-olds he'd comforted when they were homesick, and even how he felt self-conscious around Theo at first, but then realized he was the biggest nerd of all. Max had a great sense of humor, as it turned out, and really appreciated all of Penny's tips about how to roast the perfect marshmallow.

Penny remembered how she'd been intimidated by Max right at the beginning of the year. Suddenly that felt so, so silly. They didn't have everything in common (Penny had absolutely no desire to hang out in the woods getting mosquito bites with a bunch of crying, smelly children), but maybe they had enough to sit together at lunch every now and then.

On her way to fifth period, Hollis stopped Penny in the hallway.

"Ball chase later today?"

Penny thought about it. She didn't have plans after school. But she also really didn't feel like chasing down soccer balls. She didn't even like soccer, now that she thought about it.

"Can't today," Penny replied. Tingle, tingle. "Actually, I might be retired. From ball chasing, that is."

She expected Hollis to be pissed. Or at least dismiss her. Instead, Hollis gave her a high five. "All good things come to an end! Oh, and if Reem asks, I said nothing about her haircut. Nothing."

Hollis bounced down the hall.

Hollis, Penny could tell, was a good sport. Not unlike Max, maybe she had things in common with the soccer girls that had nothing to do with their feelings toward athletics.

Later that day Penny's substitute math teacher sent the entire class to the library. "Study hall," she'd called it as she ushered the class into the space. The sub gave Mrs. Notarino a *look* and vanished back the way from which they came, presumably to drink fifty cups of coffee in the teachers' lounge. Penny, in no mood to actually study, went for her usual library move: math book propped up as a shield, episode five of *Bakin' with Bacon* cued up on her phone.

Penny sat back, relaxed, and prepared to enjoy the free period. Ryder sat down at the table next to her. Penny felt a tingle coming on—she wasn't in the mood for him to point out her stature, especially since she was sitting and probably appeared even shorter than usual (not that he was so tall). Luckily, Ryder ignored her; he promptly put his head on the table and fell asleep. Five minutes later, his snores echoed throughout the library. Unfortunately for Ryder, no giggle, whisper, much less snore was lost on Mrs. Notarino.

"Ryder Hopkins," Mrs. Notarino scream-whispered. Busted. Ryder's eyes jerked open. "Get your behind up here. I am giving you detention for sleeping."

Sleeping. Ryder was tired. He shared a bedroom with his three younger siblings, Penny remembered from that first day with her necklace in the cafeteria. Of course he was exhausted. They probably carried on all night and wet the bed. Ryder had more on his mind than met the eye. Penny decided to do him a favor. A Secrets Necklace–inspired favor.

"Actually, it was me," Penny said.

Across the library, Mrs. Notarino narrowed her eyes in suspicion. Penny faked a yawn that quickly became a real yawn.

"Truly. I didn't sleep well last night. Zombie apocalypse nightmares were lit." Penny hoped her outrageous excuse mixed with teenage slang would confuse Mrs. Notarino enough that she'd believe her.

It did.

"That's a warning for you, Ms. Hoppe."

"Okay, won't happen again," Penny chimed, offering a smile that dripped with molasses and candy canes. To Penny's surprise, Ryder mouthed *thank you*. Penny gave him a thumbs-up.

"Hey," Penny whispered. "It's better to stand up your textbook and use that as a shield." For someone constantly tired, Ryder sure didn't have the best strategy as to how not to get caught napping. Maybe he didn't care, Penny considered. "I do it all the time so I can watch shows on my phone in here."

"You hacked the Wi-Fi?" Ryder said, suddenly perking up.

"Basically," Penny confirmed, proud to be the one in the know. "Password is *rocketpizza*, whatever that means. One word, no caps."

"Rad. You're cool. Thanks, dude."

"No prob," Penny said. Then, before turning back to her show, "Dude."

That same day after school, Penny begrudgingly extricated her geometry textbook (which she still hadn't managed to low-key misplace) from her locker when Samson and Jane marched up to her.

"Yo, Penn, what do you think is better: Gang of Compounding Scientists—" Samson asked. No, demanded.

"Or," Jane interrupted, "Fantasy Dream Scientists."

Penny laughed. Both names were ridiculous and weird. Weird in the right way.

"What about Gang of Compounding Dreams?" Penny suggested. "Or something like that. I personally think the scientist part is unnecessary."

"I *told* you," Jane said. Penny noticed that Sullivan and Janiyah weren't right behind them.

"You guys are so literal," Samson said, sulking away.

"He's, like, such an idiot. I don't know what Janiyah sees in him. Anyway, headed to the Cavern to play

Fantasy Dream blah blah blah. My life goal is to beat Samson at the ridiculous game he made up. Come find us."

Maybe I will, Penny thought as she packed the rest of her books into her backpack. "See ya there," she confirmed.

Only after a fiery speed round of Fantasy Dream House did Penny realize she'd survived the entire school day without sneezing once. For seventh grade, that was a world record.

Chapter twenty-two

Penny couldn't stop thinking about Otis. They hadn't exchanged more than a couple texts since her visit to Atlanta: She'd sent him a photo of her sprinkle-covered sick snack, and a few hours later he'd texted back, Dope. Then, feel better, GP.

Penny's instinct was to be offended. That wasn't much of a response at all. In fact, she'd say it qualified as definitely rude. But then Penny remembered his slumped shoulders, the way he sank down onto that milk crate, and everything he'd spilled about chopping potatoes and Chef. Maybe Otis deserved some slack. In fact, maybe he deserved more than that. Penny decided to do him a solid.

Penny was late to the cafeteria for lunch the next day. She'd caught Mr. Turney and Ms. Citron in the hallway positively flirting in front of the door to the teachers' lounge, and she simply could not tear her eyes away. It was weird when grown-ups flirted. Not good weird, not bad weird; just weird weird.

Gianna, Rose, and Nayeli were at the table smack in the middle of the bustling room, right where they always sat. Penny saw that her corner of the far corner table was vacant, awaiting her arrival. Brown bag of carefully prepared crudités in hand, she went up to Gianna anyway.

"Hey, Gianna."

"Hey, Penny!" Gosh. Gianna really was so nice.

"Question for you," Penny asked, helping herself to the open seat. "About Atlanta."

"Home sweet home," Gianna said wistfully, placing her hand over her heart. In that moment, Penny understood exactly why she found Gianna's "Where I'm From" poem to be so captivating. "What's up?"

"Do you know any good places to eat on Buford Highway?"

Gianna beamed, as if this was the question she'd been waiting for all along. "Altagracia's has the best Mexican in the Southeast."

"You used to go there a lot?"

"Duh. It's my step-grandma's restaurant!" For the

second time when it came to Gianna King, Penny's mind was officially blown.

"Wait a second. You have a restaurant in your family?"

"Yup."

"And a step-grandma?"

"Yup."

"What's so crazy about a step-grandma?" Nayeli asked. "I have a real grandma."

"Different," Penny and Gianna said at the same time. They looked at each other and giggled.

"Why do you ask?" Gianna said.

"My brother, he's a cook." Penny paused. Was that still true? Yes. Yes, it was. Even if Otis was doing more dishwashing than grilling, even if he worked out of their home kitchen and not Aujourd'hui, he was still a cook. Always and forever. *I should tell him that*, Penny thought. "Yes, he's a cook. Anyway, he's been checking out Buford Highway to try all the different cuisines. He lives in Atlanta now."

"Jealous."

"Me too." Then Penny took a risk. "He just moved there. Probably right when you moved up here, actually. It's been a bummer since he left."

Penny sneezed.

"Bless you," Gianna said. "Allergies here are insane."

"Hey, we're going to get more cheese fries," Rose interrupted. Penny had completely forgotten Rose and Nayeli were at the table. "Want?"

"Sure," Penny and Gianna, again, replied in unison.

"BRB," they chimed.

Once Rose and Nayeli were out of eavesdropping distance, Penny admitted, "That's not it. The allergies. I sneeze when I'm nervous, I think." Could it be allergies, too?

"You know, as the new kid this year, I feel like I got a fresh perspective on everything, and I have to admit I never would have guessed you were nervous."

"Impossible," Penny said, astonished. "I'm like a walking, sneezing advertisement for being nervous." *Or, at least that's what it feels like*, she thought.

"True story!" Gianna insisted. "The opposite, actually. You come across as so confident and sure of yourself. Like you are perfectly happy just to do your own thing, like you don't need anyone. I could never. Very impressive. Honestly, you are kind of intimidating."

Mind. Blown.

"Wow. I had no idea."

"I guess the outside doesn't always match the inside," Gianna said, blushing a bit. She took a sip out of her water bottle.

"Sure doesn't," Penny agreed.

Rose and Nayeli arrived with two dishes of cheese fries. "Lullwater's finest," Nayeli said.

The girls dug into the fries. Penny took out her vegetables—carrot sticks, broccoli, and, of course, mini corn, and dipped them into the excess cheese.

"Solid veggie haul," Rose noted. "Love a carrot stick."

"Or as the French would say—" Penny joked.

"Crudités," Gianna said, finished her sentence. Yes, the girls who both secretly thought they were the most nervous kids at Lullwater Middle School had much more in common than their anxieties, as it turned out.

Lunch soon came to an end and it was time for Penny to head to geometry.

"I'm going to tell Otis to go to your step-grandma's spot. What should he get?"

"Mole. Family recipe from Oaxaca. Negro and rojo are the most popular, but tell him the coloradito is my favorite. It's on the secret menu."

Penny smiled, and Gianna smiled right back. It was then that Penny realized why Gianna was so popular. It wasn't because she had perfect hair or that she was so nice. Well, those qualities didn't hurt. But that wasn't it. Gianna was easy to talk to, easy to be with, easy to get to know. She shared herself. Penny enjoyed spending time with someone like that. Just being around Gianna gave Penny an additional spark of courage for herself.

Penny texted Otis on her way to math class, careful to make sure Mr. Turney was nowhere in sight.

Dude. Altagracia's on Buford. Order coloradito off the secret menu. Party in your mouth.

Otis responded a few minutes later right as Penny sat down at her desk. Oh yeah? I hear it's bomb.

It is, Penny wrote back, without any hesitation. She trusted Gianna.

"Did you read it?" was all Penny said when Lark placed her long-lost poetry journal in her hands. The girls stood in the Cavern after school. Lark had found it by the athletic field that day Penny earned her title as ball-chaser extraordinaire. It must have fallen out of Penny's backpack in the shuffle. Lark explained that she liked to go out there on that hill to draw. Something about how the light filtered through the trees. Very not New York City, which was a bummer but also interesting from an artistic perspective.

"I didn't know who it belonged to. It didn't say your name or anything, just 'Chef.'" Lark blushed and looked at her feet. She wore a surprisingly large shoe size. "But yeah. I did." A wave of sparks careened to Penny's nose. "I'm sorry. That wasn't right. I thought maybe there would be a clue inside and then I could find the rightful owner, but after reading I still couldn't figure it out. I really wasn't trying to snoop. Your 'Where I'm From' poem was so interesting that once I started I couldn't stop. I stole your secrets. I'm sorry."

Penny squeezed her poetry journal a little tighter. It felt good to have it in her hands again.

"I can't blame you," Penny said finally. "Secrets are very tempting."

"I drew this thing—an illustration, I guess—if it makes you feel any better. I might submit it to the paper again. Only if that's cool." Lark took her sketchbook from her backpack. "The line about the magnolia tree made me feel like I could see it. When I feel like I can see something without actually looking at it with my eyes, that's when I know it's worth drawing."

Lark opened the sketchbook to the last page and held it out for Penny, and anyone within visual eavesdropping distance, to see.

Of course, Lark had never been to Penny's backyard, so the illustration was technically a little off. In real life the branches started lower to the ground and the leaves weren't as thick at the top. But at the same time, Lark's drawing also looked exactly like Penny's magnolia tree. She managed to capture how Penny felt when she sat on her bat wing–shaped branch. The illustration was just right.

"My tree," Penny whispered, just loud enough for both her and Lark to hear.

"I didn't quite know where you fit in, so maybe it's not done yet. I'm not sure. But you can have it if you want. As a trade for letting me read your poem. Even though you didn't mean to or know I was reading it." Lark looked down at her big feet. "Okay, I've made it weird now."

"Good weird," Penny replied. She smiled at Lark,

with her teeth. "Submit it to the newspaper. It's really . . ." Penny racked her brain for the perfect word. "Alive."

I stole your secrets. The phrase stuck with Penny the rest of the day. It occurred to Penny that Lark reading her poetry journal wasn't all that different than what her Secrets Necklace had allowed her to do these past few weeks. Not that different at all.

Yes, people loved Gianna because she was open. She let herself smile and gave generous hugs. Lark and Gianna were so different, but Penny liked them both. Neither girl was afraid to share the things they cared about, the things that made them who they were.

Maybe, Penny considered, she'd been thinking about the information her Secrets Necklace gave her incorrectly all along. The last step of the vanished recipe said to listen. How could Penny expect people to listen to her if she didn't offer anything for them to hear? As Lark might say, Penny had stolen a lot of secrets. Maybe it was time to share some of her own.

Chapter twenty-three

The early evening sun cast a glowy haze into the kitchen. Penny's favorite cooking light. She hadn't given up on Project Better than the Box. Not yet.

"Thirty-four down. Four letters. 'Traditional Mexican dish with upwards of twenty ingredients.'"

"You're not trying to cheat, are you, Sylvia?" Penny chided. She scooped three cups of flour and combined it with the sugar and baking powder. Butter melted slowly on the stove. Penny wasn't going to rely on a microwave. That felt too hands-off.

"I ain't cheating. I'm asking for help. As long as I ask you and not the internet, that's not cheating. You should know this by now," Sylvia scolded, but Penny smiled. Sylvia was . . . weird. Not good weird—*great* weird.

Penny mixed the dry ingredients and took the melted butter off the stove. She added a dash of vanilla, not bothering to measure out a teaspoon exactly. Then another for good measure. Vanilla was delicious.

"Rojo. Negro. Verde."

"Lots of clues, Sylvia. Are you sure that's a cross-word puzzle for adults and not the junior version?"

"Don't start with me," Sylvia challenged. Penny giggled. It was fun to rile Sylvia up.

She cracked two eggs into the butter mixture and whisked the ingredients to combine. One more room-temperature egg rested on the counter next to the bowl.

"And coloradito," Sylvia added. "Any guesses?"

"What if my brain actually *is* the internet? You know that's how it works now, right?" Penny teased. She wasn't convinced Sylvia knew exactly what the internet was, to be honest.

Sylvia snorted.

Penny considered the extra egg. Most recipes called for either two or three eggs. But then again, none of those recipes had worked. Penny remembered what Sylvia said the other day. *Sometimes recipes are meant to be broken.* Penny had an idea. An untraditional idea. She picked up the third egg and cracked it on the counter. Careful not to let any of the contents spill just yet, she held the two shells over the bowl. Slowly, so not to make a mistake, but not all that concerned if she did, Penny managed to add half of the egg white and half of the yolk to the batter. Two and a half eggs.

Penny sat with Sylvia as the cake baked. Most of the crossword was completed, though the four-letter answer to thirty-four down remained empty. A mouth-watering aroma filled the air. The smell reminded Penny of birthdays and special breakfasts and the bat wing–shaped branch on her magnolia tree. And Otis.

Penny looked over Sylvia's shoulder at the puzzle. *Traditional Mexican dish with upwards of twenty ingredients. Rojo, negro, verde, coloradito.*

Of course! Penny knew the answer.

She gently took the pencil out of Sylvia's hand and filled in the four empty boxes. *M-O-L-E.* Sylvia huffed but also gave Penny a quick pat on the back.

Penny waited to do an official taste test until after dinner, when seven of the eight heartbeats belonging to the little yellow house on Plum Street were under one roof. Penny cut slices for Mom, Dad, Sylvia, and herself. Millions, Scraffy, and Rent would get the crumbs.

"I present to you: Project Better than the Box. Attempt number . . ."

"One million!" Sylvia cackled, pointing to the lizard tank and winking.

"Sure. Attempt number one million."

She thought about what Otis had said behind the restaurant that night. About his favorite part of cooking: making food for others to enjoy and sharing himself. Not unlike her "Where I'm From" poem, Penny had poured her heart plus two and a half eggs into that cake.

As Penny raised the fork to her mouth, she realized it didn't matter if that cake was better than the box. Maybe that wasn't the point. Now, in addition to the birthdays and that Christmas morning, she'd have a memory of sharing her special two-and-a-half-egg cake with seven of her eight favorite heartbeats in the whole entire world. That sounded like a sure win to Penny Hoppe.

Chapter twenty-four

The next morning on the way to Tina's Treasures, Penny texted Otis.

Dude. 7th grade is a handful. I haven't learned a lot because in case you forgot, 7th grade is mostly ridiculous. I do know one thing: What you think people are thinking and what they're actually thinking are never really the same. And more than likely it has nothing to do with you. Words of wisdom from the one and only Ghost Pepp.

Oh, and don't worry about me. If you quit and come home, I'll pee in your soft scrambled eggs.

"I'm glad you came with me, Penny girl," Mom said when Penny'd put her phone away. Mom had left her headset at home, Penny noticed.

"Me too." *I have something I need to give back*, Penny thought. And then, because there was no way for Mom to know if she didn't tell her, "I have something I need to give back, too."

Just then, the opening chords of a Heat Squad classic came on the radio.

"Turn it up!" Penny said.

Together, Penny and her mom sang at the top of their lungs the rest of the car ride.

"No returns, but especially no partial returns. Jeans without pockets? A hoodie without a hood? Would you give back a watermelon without its seeds?" Roxanna asked sarcastically.

Though Penny suspected the questions were rhetorical, she still considered possible answers.

"No box, no necklace, no returns, no thank you." Roxanna picked up her book. The cover concealing her face, Penny saw a very familiar title.

"What is *Honestly, Jacques* about, anyway?" Penny asked.

"Everything," Roxanna answered without missing a beat.

Roxanna was a weirdo. Possibly in the very best way.

Oh well, Penny thought, tucking the broken necklace back into her pocket. She would just keep it. Mom could take her somewhere to get the chain fixed. Even without its magic power, the key-shaped charm wasn't bad-looking on its own. After quickly perusing the kitchen aisle (nothing new since her last visit) Penny wandered to the back office. She was getting antsy.

"Mom, you ready?"

"Hey, you, I know you're not coming in here without saying hi to me first," Tina said, already wrapping Penny in a hug.

"Hey, Miss Tina," Penny said, her voice muffled in Tina's shoulder. She smelled like caramel popcorn.

"Penny girl, I'll tell you what: You hang up these jackets over on the winter rack, and your mama will take you to Bendy's on the way home."

"That's a bribe, Miss Tina," Penny said.

"It certainly is."

Penny looked at her mom, who said, "When at Tina's, I play by her rules."

"Deal," Penny agreed, grabbing the half dozen winter coats already on hangers and dashing out of the office. She noticed her old coat was at the top of the pile. Penny had an idea.

She hung up her coat last. *To make up for the syrup stain*, she thought. Quickly, in case Roxanna was watching, Penny slipped the key-shaped charm and the busted chain into the jacket's pocket. Penny had officially outgrown both items.

"Bye, Roxanna, love," Mom called as they walked by the register a few minutes later.

"See ya. Love ya; don't mean it."

"You *do* mean it!" Penny exclaimed, pointing at Roxanna as if she'd caught her red-handed.

Roxanna rolled her eyes and returned to her book. Roxanna was hard on the outside, but as Penny had learned, that didn't mean she wasn't soft and sweet in the middle. Penny gazed over her shoulder and blew Roxanna a kiss, and Roxanna's mouth, as if against her will, twitched into the slightest smile.

Chapter twenty-five

Spark, spark, spark.

Tingle, tingle, tingle.

Spark, tingle, spark, tingle.

Penny stood in line backstage with her classmates. Onstage, Penny heard Mateo introduce himself.

"Hi, I'm Mateo Pinzon, and my poem is called 'Where I'm From.'" His voice only cracked a little at the end. So far, everybody—including Gianna, who was the third to read—had titled their poems "Where I'm From."

Penny was next. Spark-tingle combo platter.

Penny couldn't see the audience from the wings, but she could sense them. The auditorium felt heavier than it had that day in dress rehearsal. Mom, Dad, and even Sylvia were somewhere out there. If she were being honest with herself, Dad had probably brought at least one lizard in his pocket. "They can't miss all the fun!" he always explained when he took reptiles to special events.

Truly, Penny thought the day of the final poetry reading would never come. Not just because she'd been dreading it for weeks, but given the way seventh grade had started, she figured she'd sneeze herself inside out beforehand.

Mateo's voice carried backstage. Penny listened. *"I'm from driveway basketball and an unstoppable jump shot."*

Penny thought about Cole and the way words smashed together like a circus, not sentences, in his brain.

Spark, spark, spark, tingle, tingle, tingle.

She thought about the shy girl who wanted to be a rock star, the sleep-deprived bully, and all the peers she'd heard think they were way too nervous, way too uncool or way too something.

Spark, smaller spark, tingle, tingle.

She thought about Gianna's step-grandma's mole and Lark bopping down the street with her lime green headphones in New York City.

Spark, tiny tingle.

And Penny thought about the very last thing her

Secrets Necklace had allowed her to hear. *I wish I knew more about her . . .*

Tingle. Spark.

Applause. Mateo was done. Penny's turn.

She took one step out of the wings, and then another, and then another. Ms. Samich was right—the lights were so bright that she couldn't see the audience. She heard them breathing, whispering, existing. She imagined most, not all, were watching her. She had no idea what any of them were thinking.

Penny arrived at the microphone. This time, it wasn't too tall for her. Sweat collected beneath her bangs. Perhaps she'd always run hot.

Mini spark, smaller tingle. *Oh well*, Penny thought. At the end of the day, a sneeze wasn't the worst thing in the world.

Penny looked down at her poem one last time. Three stanzas, twelve lines. The words on the page were personal and private and perfect and true. They were alive.

One final spark, one last tingle.

Penny took a deep breath and began.

"'My Secret Ingredients: A recipe by Penny H.'"

Chapter Twenty-Six

Four hours after the poetry reading, Penny sat in the magnolia tree. She balanced the wooden recipe box on her lap, using the hard surface to lean against as she wrote a letter to Otis on the backside of a blank recipe card. Though the letter wasn't quite poetry, writing her words on the page was a little easier than saying them out loud, and more dramatic than a text. Penny, both in the kitchen and in poetry readings, sometimes had a flair for the dramatic.

The sun was starting to set earlier in the day; it was already dusk. Fireflies were long gone for the season, so it was just Penny alone, perched on the branch that reminded her of a bat wing, protected by a fortress of leaves. Though Penny now had a bit more experience sharing herself, she still treasured her privacy.

After the poetry reading, several of her class-mates came up to her to comment on her poem.

"I didn't realize you were so into cooking. That's so cool!" Janiyah said.

"We were thinking . . . science is back on," Samson said. "Doing a fantasy-dream-house-and-cooking-experiment thing this weekend. You can teach us about the cooking part, yeah?" he mentioned, some-where between asking and demanding.

Gianna gave her a gigantic hug (they really were as good as advertised), then introduced Penny to her step-grandma, who had traveled all the way from Atlanta for the event.

Immediately after Penny got offstage, Lark gave her a smile and two thumbs up. Ms. Samich even squeezed Penny's shoulder. The touch proved so comforting that Penny wondered if she would ever sneeze again.

Penny still missed Otis. But she also had Lark's number newly stored in her phone and plans with Gianna to test their hands at a never-before-attempted Thai curry later that week. Finally, there was more to seventh grade than missing her brother.

Dad was making dinner that night. "Grilled cheese and a surprise to celebrate." Penny thought to inquire and then advise about his cooking technique, but decided against it. She was curious to see what he came up with.

Penny glanced up from her letter in progress. Ashy light filtered through the magnolia leaves. She leaned her head against the trunk. She could smell the moss all the way from the driveway.

She'd pack her letter inside the recipe box and send it to Otis. He'd probably never gotten mail at his new address, Penny realized. She hoped that if Otis ever doubted the fact that he was a real cook, he could look at that box and remember where he was from.

Dude,

Box cake isn't good because it's the best-tasting cake in the world. It's delicious because of my fifth birthday when the candle melted into the icing and I got a mouthful of wax, and on Christmas when we ate it for breakfast before Mom and Dad woke up, and even in the magnolia tree the day before you moved to Atlanta. Box cake is the best because of who you share it with, not because of the taste.

Anyway, I figured out the recipe. It's on the other side. Enjoy, weirdo.

Love,

Ghost Pepper

Penny flipped the card. Now complete, printed in her careful handwriting, her work perfectly described the inside of her heart and soul. Penny read her words one last time.

My Secret Ingredients: A Recipe by Penny H.
I am from a little yellow house on Plum Street,
Eight heartbeats under one roof.
I am from the bat wing branch of my magnolia tree,
A kingdom filled with fireflies where I eat (better-than-the) box cake for breakfast.

I'm from crudités, ladles, and cast-iron skillets,
Soft scrambled eggs and cook the garlic on low for thirty seconds or until fragrant.

I'm from a pocket full of lizards, twinkling gold hoops,
aujourd'hui, and tomorrow,
46 across, 23 down, no cheating allowed.

I'm also from sparks and tingles,
Sneezes and so many nerves.
Will life go back to normal with Otis in Atlanta,
Or is normal just a recipe that's meant to be broken?

A fantasy dream house full of Peanut Butter Lovers,
sprinkles, and no geometry books in sight,
I'm from a preheated oven, Ghost Pepper hot,
Not two eggs, not three,
But somewhere in between.

Acknowledgments

Thank you to the Scholastic team: David Levithan, Yaffa Jaskoll, Nora Milman, Courtney Vincento, Susan Hom. A heartfelt thank-you to everyone who had a hand in making this book whole. And the (not-so) secret ingredient: Orlando Dos Reis, editor supreme. Thank you for your generous trust in my voice, ideas, and ability to make deadlines.

Way back in seventh grade, I never suspected I'd be writing books, but boy oh boy do my friendships born in Paideia Jr. High (and before) make the process all the more enjoyable. Boom, Katie, Steph, Casey, Log, Julia, Karimah, Evan, Mike, Blake, Mitch, Jam: Y'all are the source of memories and laughs that hopefully fill the pages of many more tales to come.

My New York fantasy dream squad: Teach, Tom, Max, Theo, Silva, Ryan, Micalizzi. Wouldn't trade y'all for all the magic necklaces in the world.

Thank you to the most patient and supportive literary wing-people: Megan O'Brien, Ham Paddock, Momma Schwartz PhD, and JP2.

Ginger Chef: Thank you for teaching me about tweezer food, mandoline slicers, peeling garlic and every kitchen move in between.

Marj, Marv, Marla (what a hitter): Cheers to bad pitches forever. Your feedback and laughter make the moments of panic all the more manageable. Thanks for always answering the phone.

My former students of PS90, PS279, and PS132: Thank you for sharing your imaginations so freely, using your voices, and always, always, always keepin' it weird.

And finally, the three other heartbeats from the yellow house on Lullwater: Momma, Dad, and Ham. Thank you, thank you. Y'all keep my heart curious, cared for, and full.

About the Author

Jessie Paddock holds a BFA in Drama from NYU's Tisch School of the Arts and an MFA in writing for children from The New School. She has lived in New York City for a while now, although she sometimes misses her hometown of Atlanta. She loves to play soccer and ride her bike to places she's never been. This is her third novel.

Read on for a sneak peek of

The Crush Necklace!

It wasn't until Moni burst through the recreation center's double doors that tears finally exploded from her eyes. The night was quiet and the air thick, like a rotten milkshake. All she could hear was the faint bass of indistinguishable music coming from inside. And now, her own sobs, too, as Grace's words played on a loop in Moni's head:

Two weirdos who nobody even likes.

It started to drizzle.

Two hours earlier, Moni had hoped that her second Friday Night Skate would be an evening she wouldn't soon forget. Now, as the light rain turned to massive drops and her tears streamed from her eyes with almost equal ferocity, Moni wished she could erase everything about seventh grade.

She looked back at the royal blue doors behind her. Nobody had followed her outside. Not Johnny, and certainly not Grace. Moni thought back to the first time she had walked into that building with her neon windbreaker, acid-washed jeans, and specks of glitter twinkling around her indigo blue eyes. She thought about what she and Grace had discovered at the end of that night.

Moni shivered. Thunder rumbled overhead. The rain didn't stop.

She walked all the way home through the storm, neither avoiding nor searching for puddles. Her once-perky half ponytail sagged from the weight of the water, and her coarse denim jeans clung to her thighs. Though it was warm for October, her teeth chattered.

In her right hand was a necklace with a key-shaped charm—the cause of all this mess. She clutched it so tightly that the grooves on the key threatened to break the skin of her palm. The broken silver chain dangled through her fingers. The stone on the charm continued to churn and swirl, like a storm in the night.

By the time Moni arrived home, soaked to the bone and too tired to sob any longer, the stone became a flat, empty black.

But Moni had yet to notice.